Cici #2

A Fairy's Tale

⸻ TRUTH IN SIGHT ⸻

Written by
Cori Doerrfeld

Illustrated by
Tyler Page and Cori Doerrfeld

GRAPHIC UNIVERSE™ · MINNEAPOLIS

Graphic Universe™
A division of Lerner Publishing Group, Inc.
241 First Avenue North
Minneapolis, MN 55401 USA

For reading levels and more information, look up this title at www.lernerbooks.com.

Main body text set in CCDaveGibbonsLower 10/11.
Typeface provided by ComicCraft.

Library of Congress Cataloging-in-Publication Data

The Cataloging-in-Publication Data for *Truth in Sight* is on file at the Library of Congress.
ISBN 978-1-4677-6153-6 (lib. bdg.)
ISBN 978-1-5124-1156-0 (pbk.)
ISBN 978-1-5124-0904-8 (EB pdf)

Manufactured in the United States of America
1 – DP – 7/15/16

For J.B.

—Cori

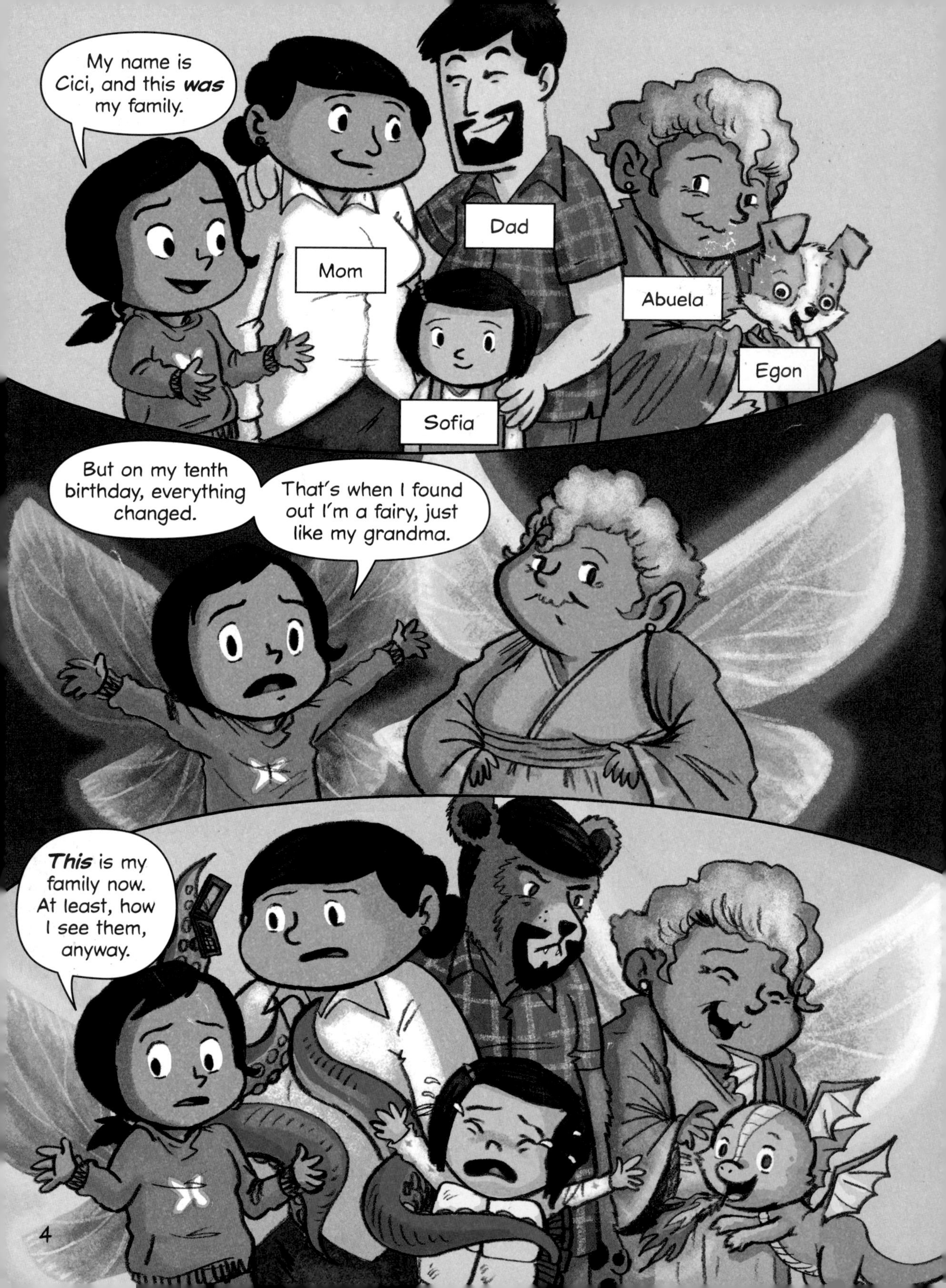
My name is Cici, and this ***was*** my family.
Mom
Dad
Abuela
Egon
Sofia
But on my tenth birthday, everything changed.
That's when I found out I'm a fairy, just like my grandma.
This is my family now. At least, how I see them, anyway.

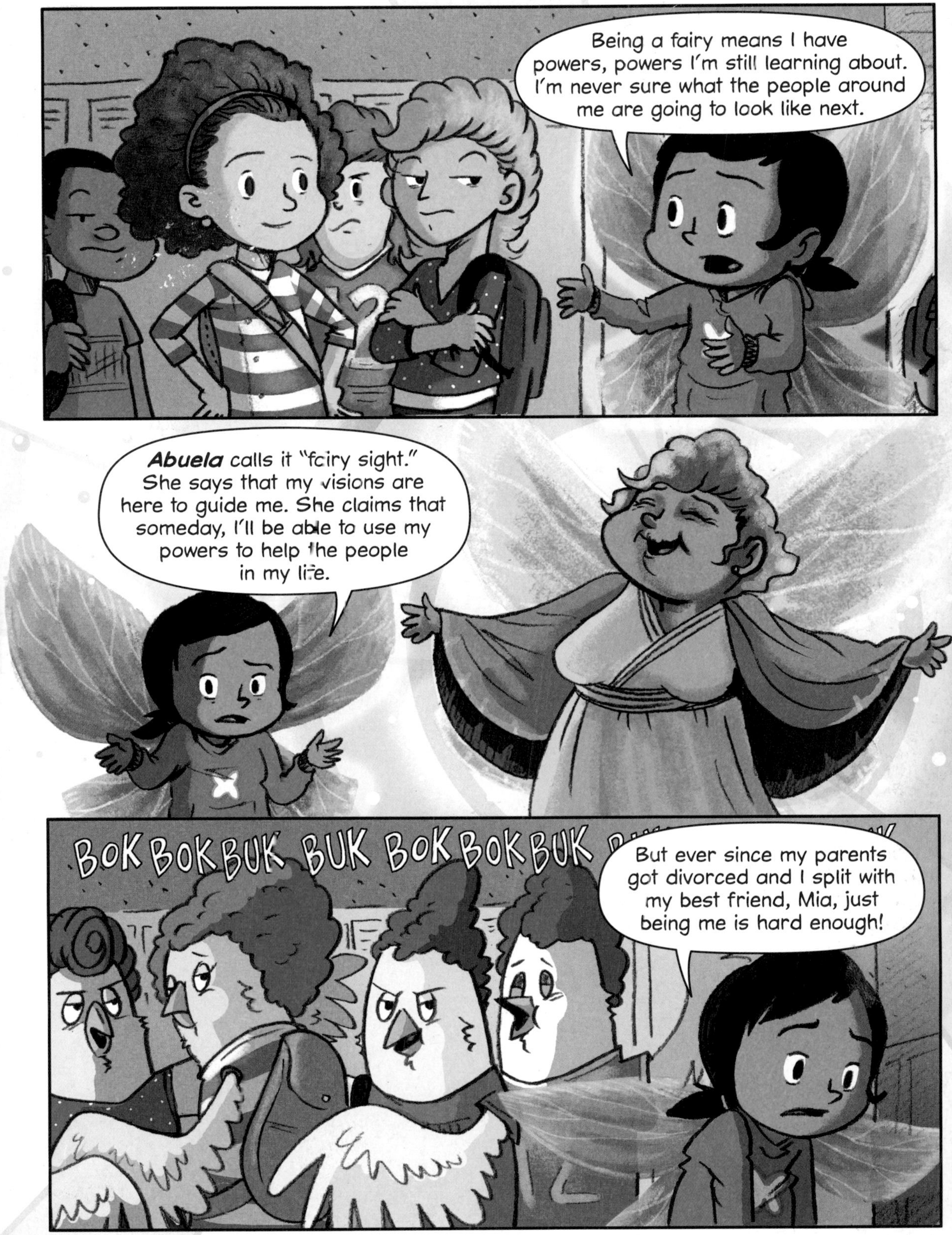
Being a fairy means I have powers, powers I'm still learning about. I'm never sure what the people around me are going to look like next.
Abuela calls it "fairy sight." She says that my visions are here to guide me. She claims that someday, I'll be able to use my powers to help the people in my life.
BOK BOK BUK BUK BOK BOK BUK
But ever since my parents got divorced and I split with my best friend, Mia, just being me is hard enough!

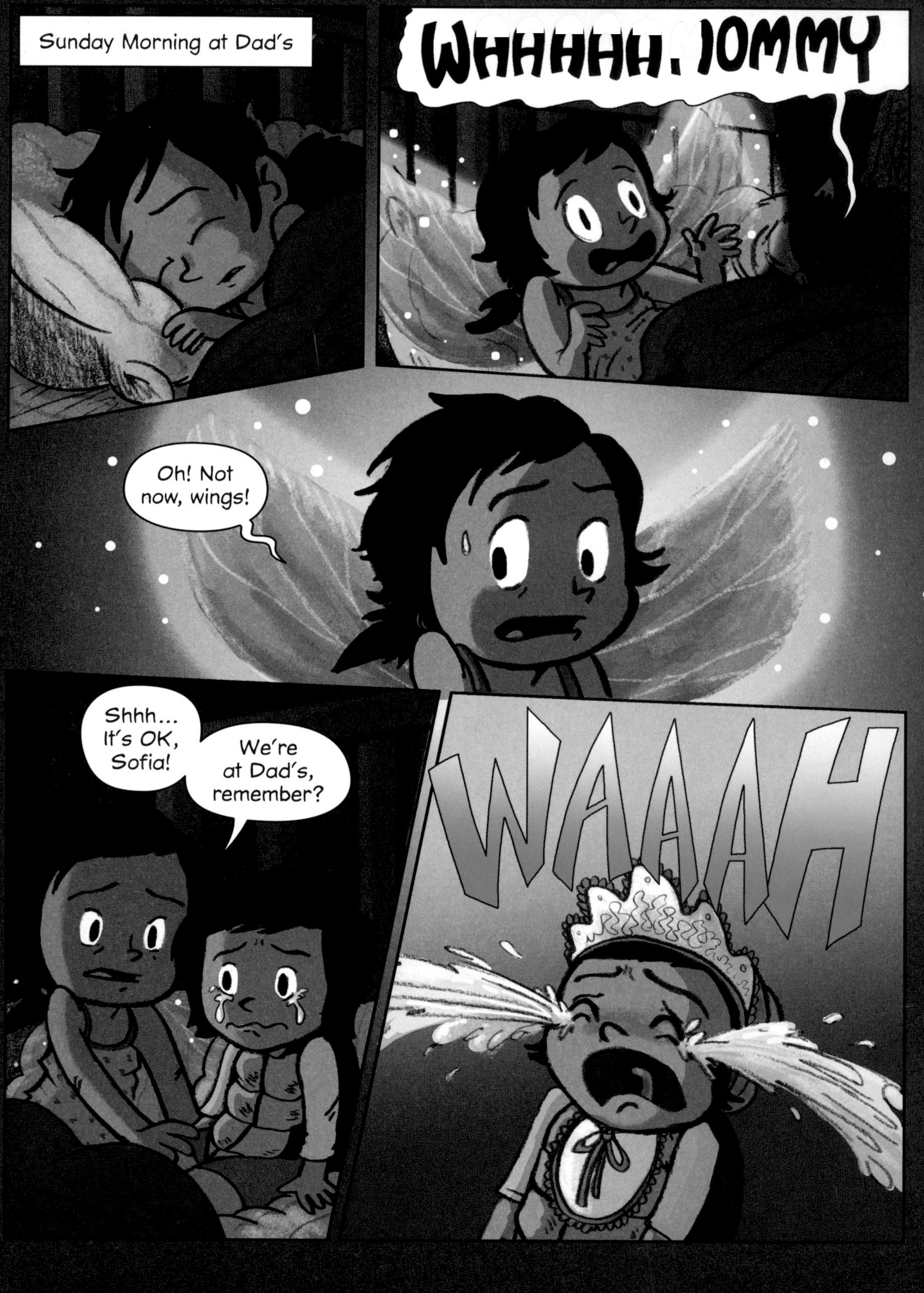
Sunday Morning at Dad's
WHHHHH. IOMMY
Oh! Not now, wings!
Shhh... It's OK, Sofia!
We're at Dad's, remember?
WAAAH

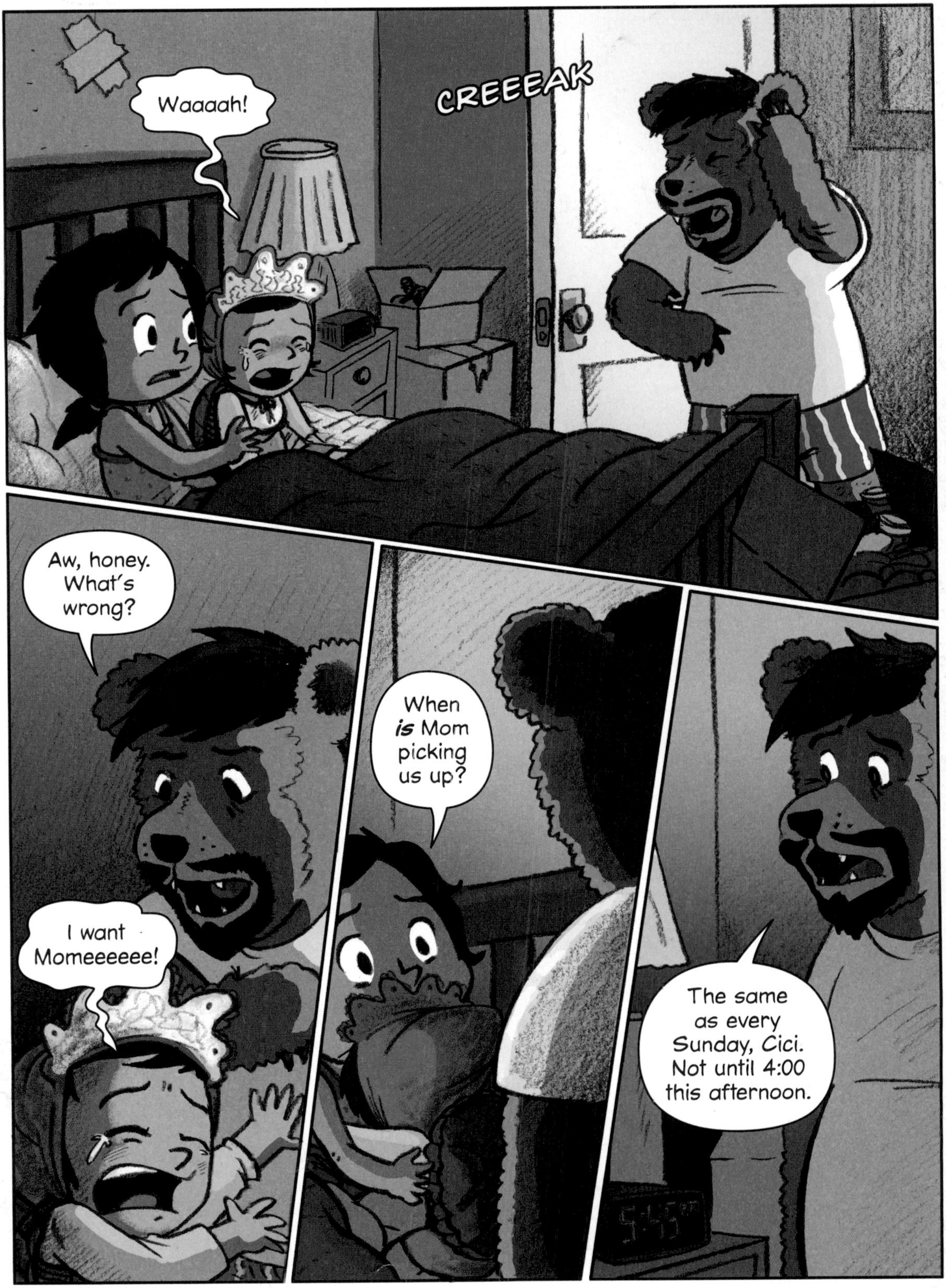

Waaaah!
CREEEEAK
Aw, honey. What's wrong?
I want Momeeeeee!
When *is* Mom picking us up?
The same as every Sunday, Cici. Not until 4:00 this afternoon.

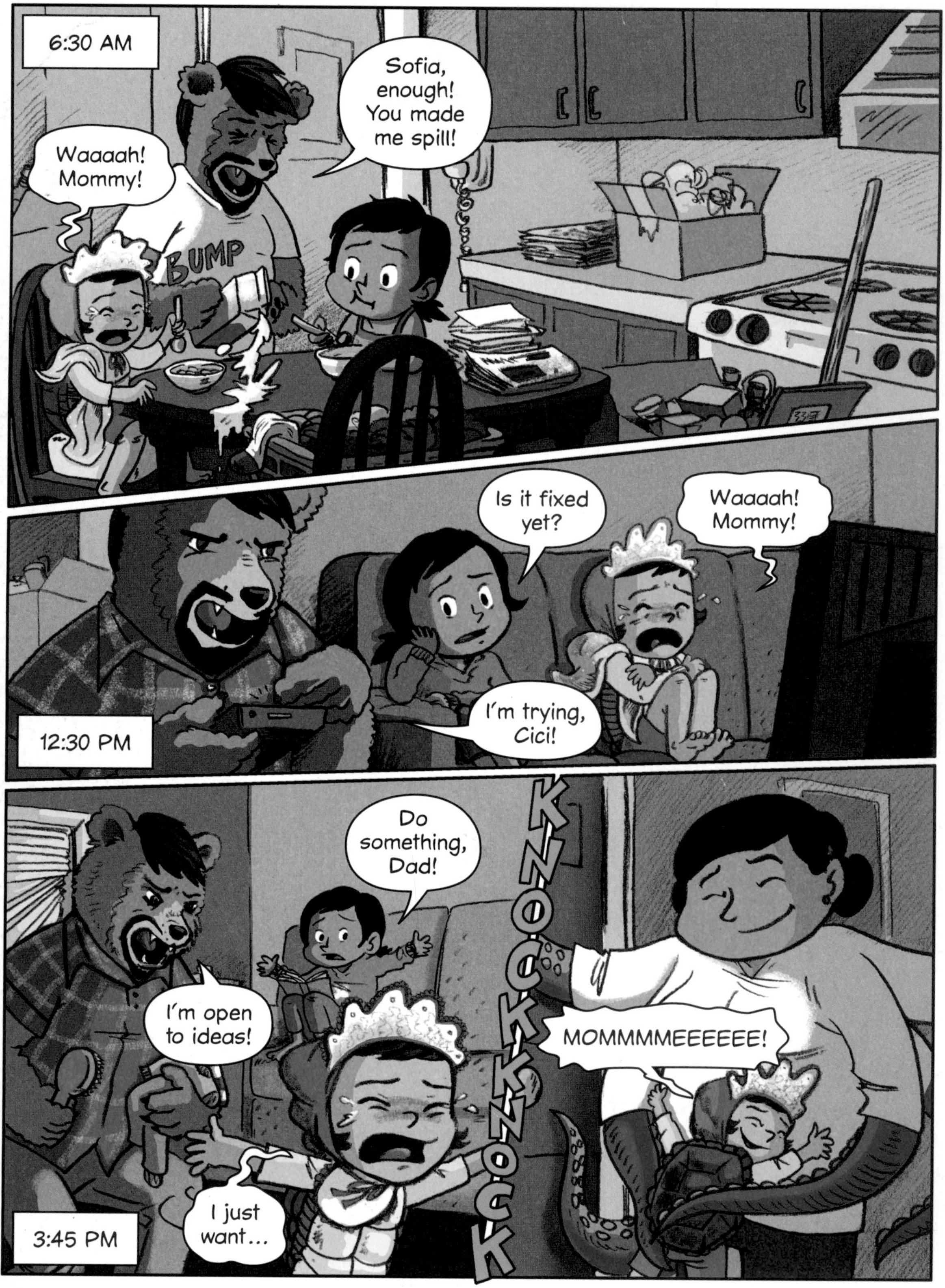
6:30 AM
Waaaah! Mommy!
Sofia, enough! You made me spill!
BUMP
Is it fixed yet?
Waaaah! Mommy!
I'm trying, Cici!
12:30 PM
Do something, Dad!
KNOCK KNOCK KNOCK
I'm open to ideas!
MOMMMMEEEEEE!
I just want...
3:45 PM

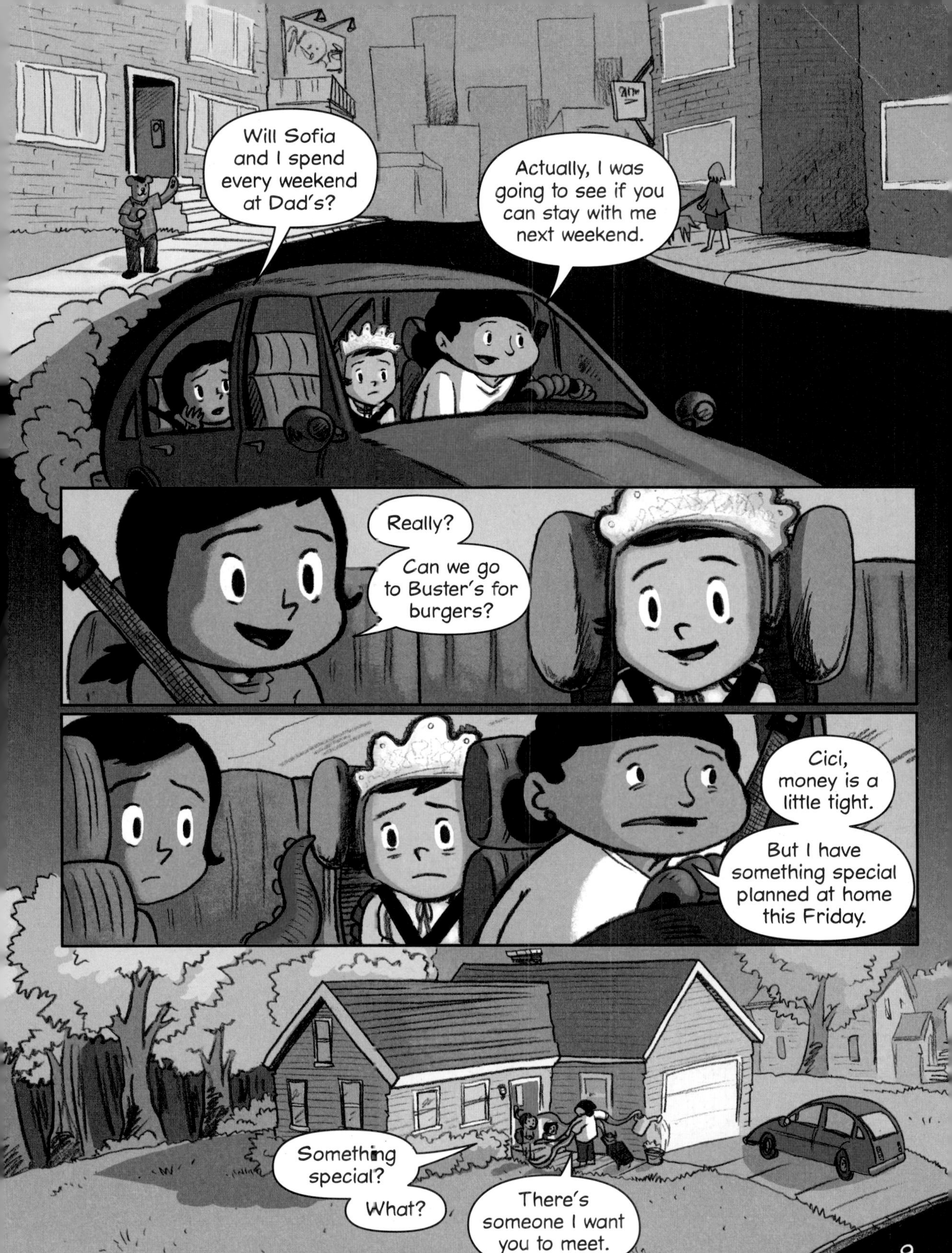
Will Sofia and I spend every weekend at Dad's?
Actually, I was going to see if you can stay with me next weekend.
Really?
Can we go to Buster's for burgers?
Cici, money is a little tight.
But I have something special planned at home this Friday.
Something special?
What?
There's someone I want you to meet.

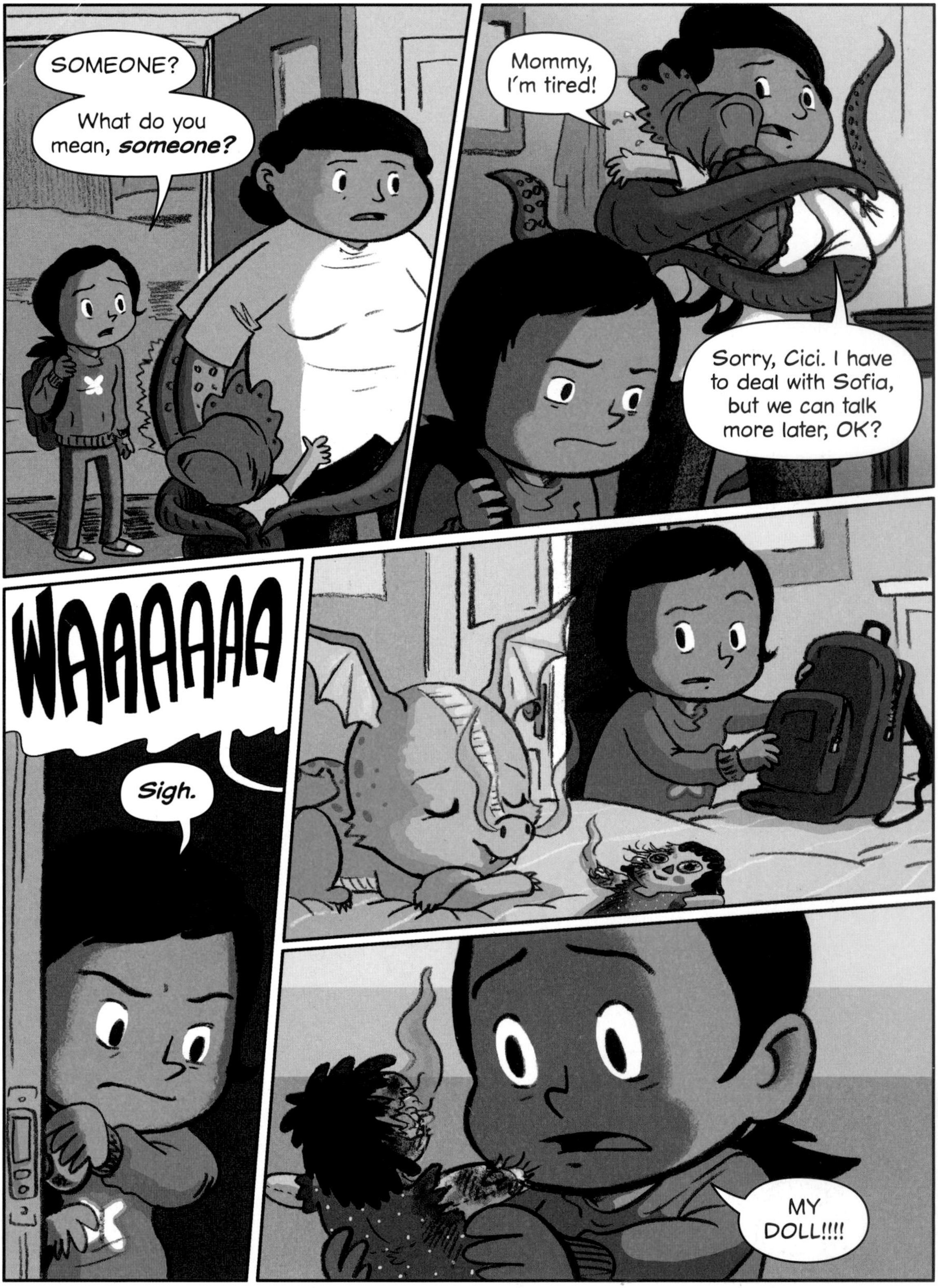
SOMEONE?
What do you mean, ***someone?***
Mommy, I'm tired!
Sorry, Cici. I have to deal with Sofia, but we can talk more later, OK?
WAAAAAA
Sigh.
MY DOLL!!!!

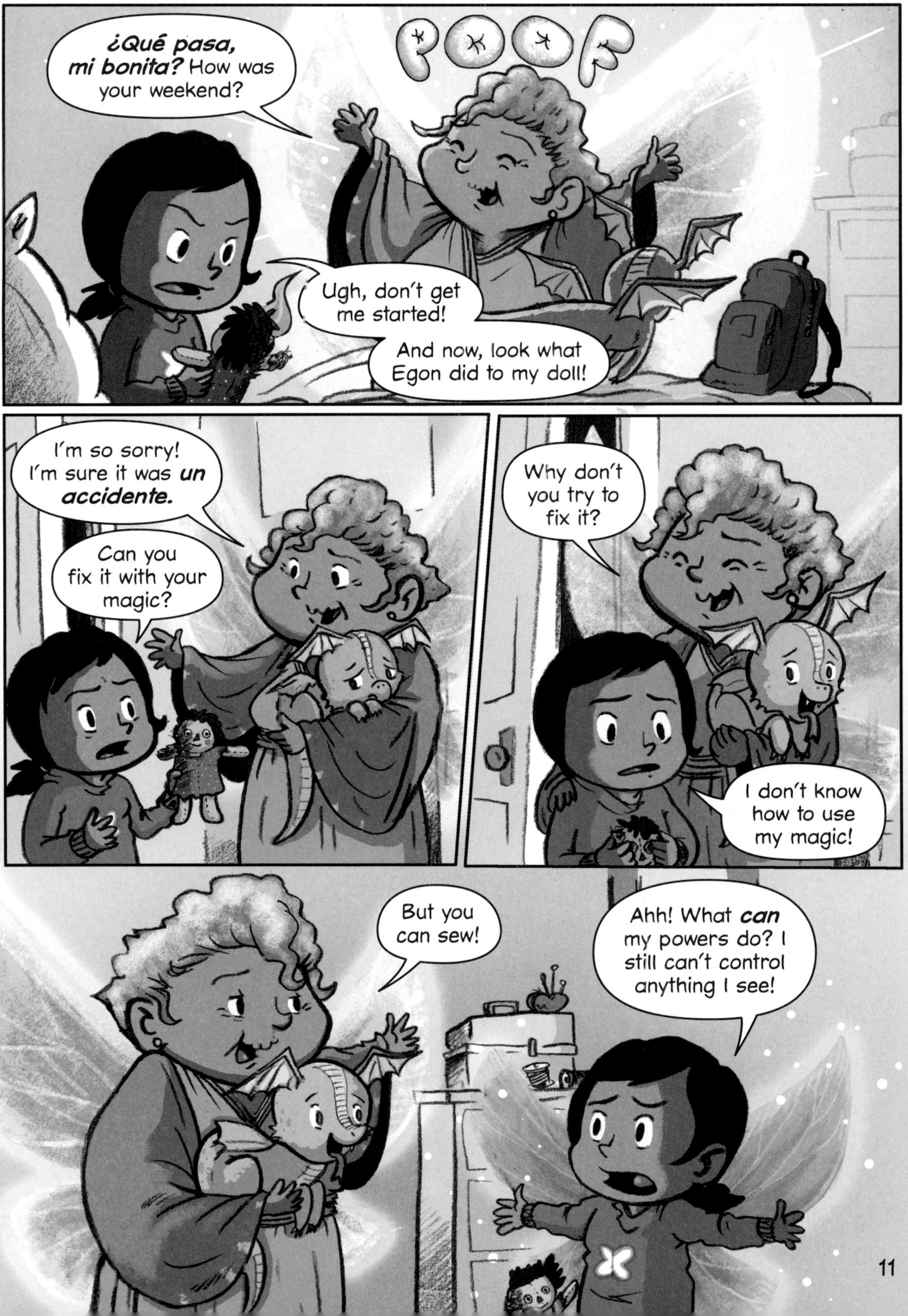
POOF
¿Qué pasa, mi bonita? How was your weekend?
Ugh, don't get me started!
And now, look what Egon did to my doll!
I'm so sorry! I'm sure it was un accidente.
Can you fix it with your magic?
Why don't you try to fix it?
I don't know how to use my magic!
But you can sew!
Ahh! What can my powers do? I still can't control anything I see!

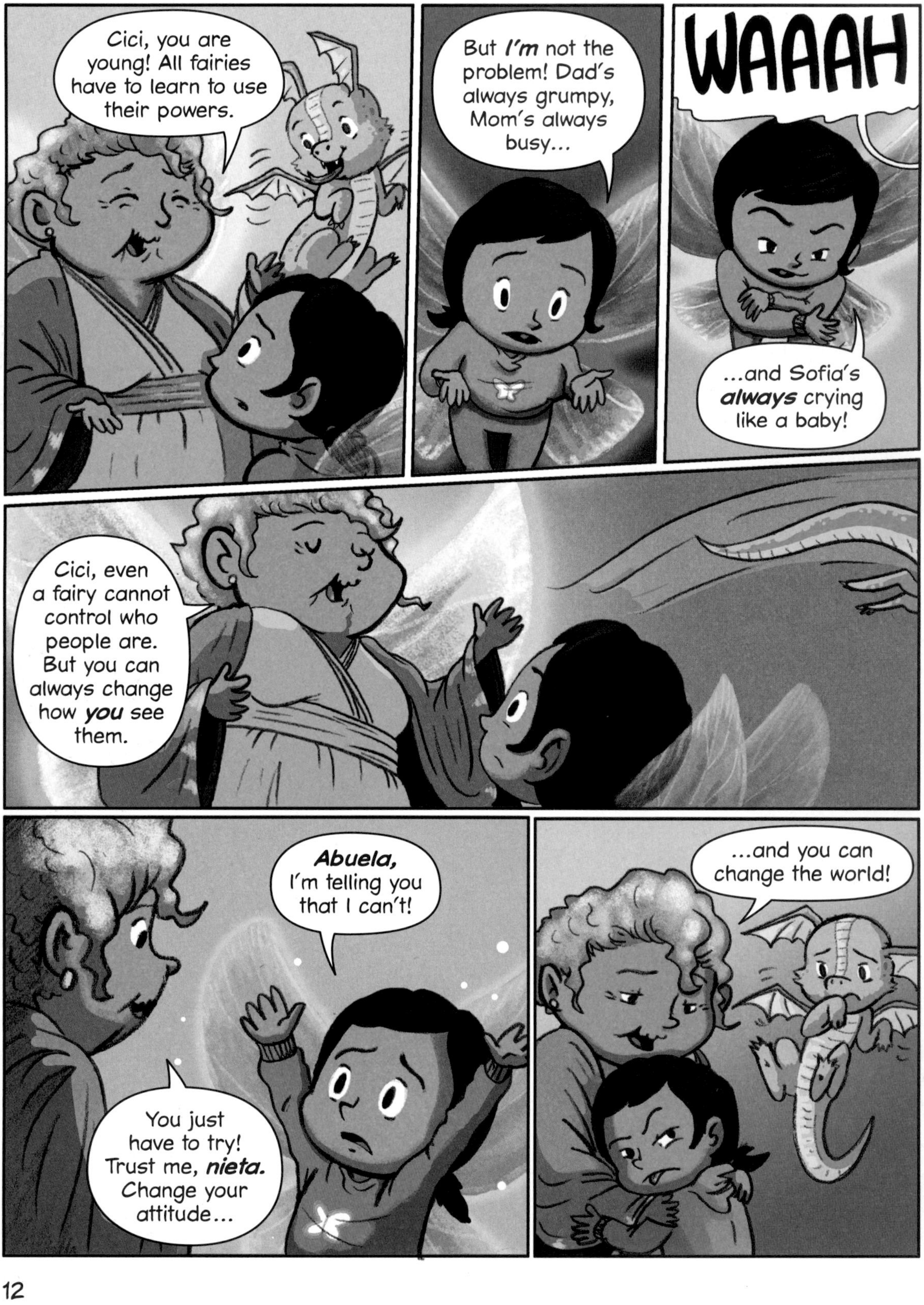
Cici, you are young! All fairies have to learn to use their powers.
But *I'm* not the problem! Dad's always grumpy, Mom's always busy...
WAAAH
...and Sofia's *always* crying like a baby!
Cici, even a fairy cannot control who people are. But you can always change how *you* see them.
Abuela, I'm telling you that I can't!
You just have to try! Trust me, *nieta.* Change your attitude...
...and you can change the world!

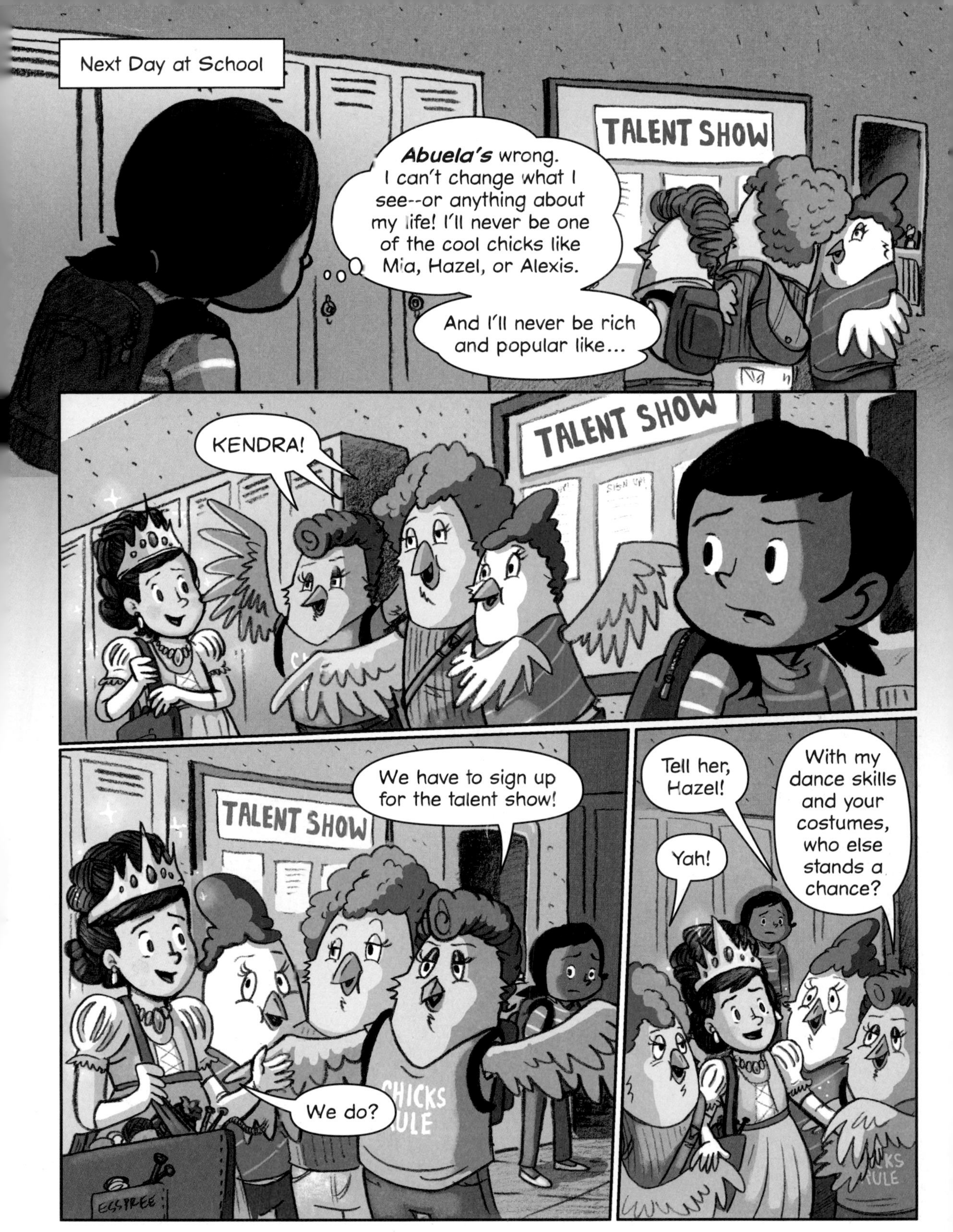

Next Day at School
TALENT SHOW
Abuela's wrong. I can't change what I see--or anything about my life! I'll never be one of the cool chicks like Mia, Hazel, or Alexis.
And I'll never be rich and popular like...
TALENT SHOW
KENDRA!
TALENT SHOW
We have to sign up for the talent show!
We do?
CHICKS RULE
Tell her, Hazel!
Yah!
With my dance skills and your costumes, who else stands a chance?

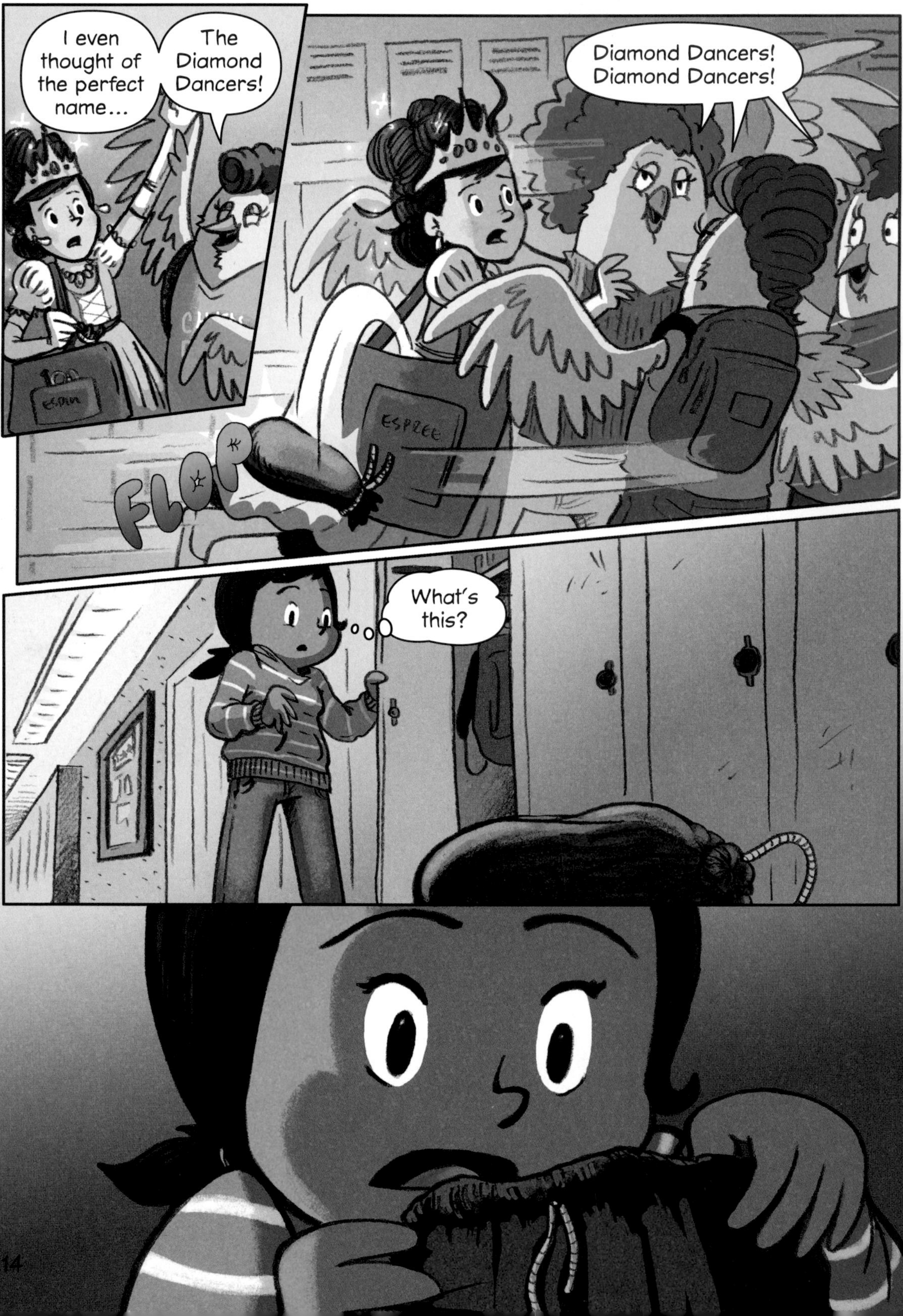
I even thought of the perfect name...
The Diamond Dancers!
Diamond Dancers! Diamond Dancers!
ESPREE
FLOP
What's this?

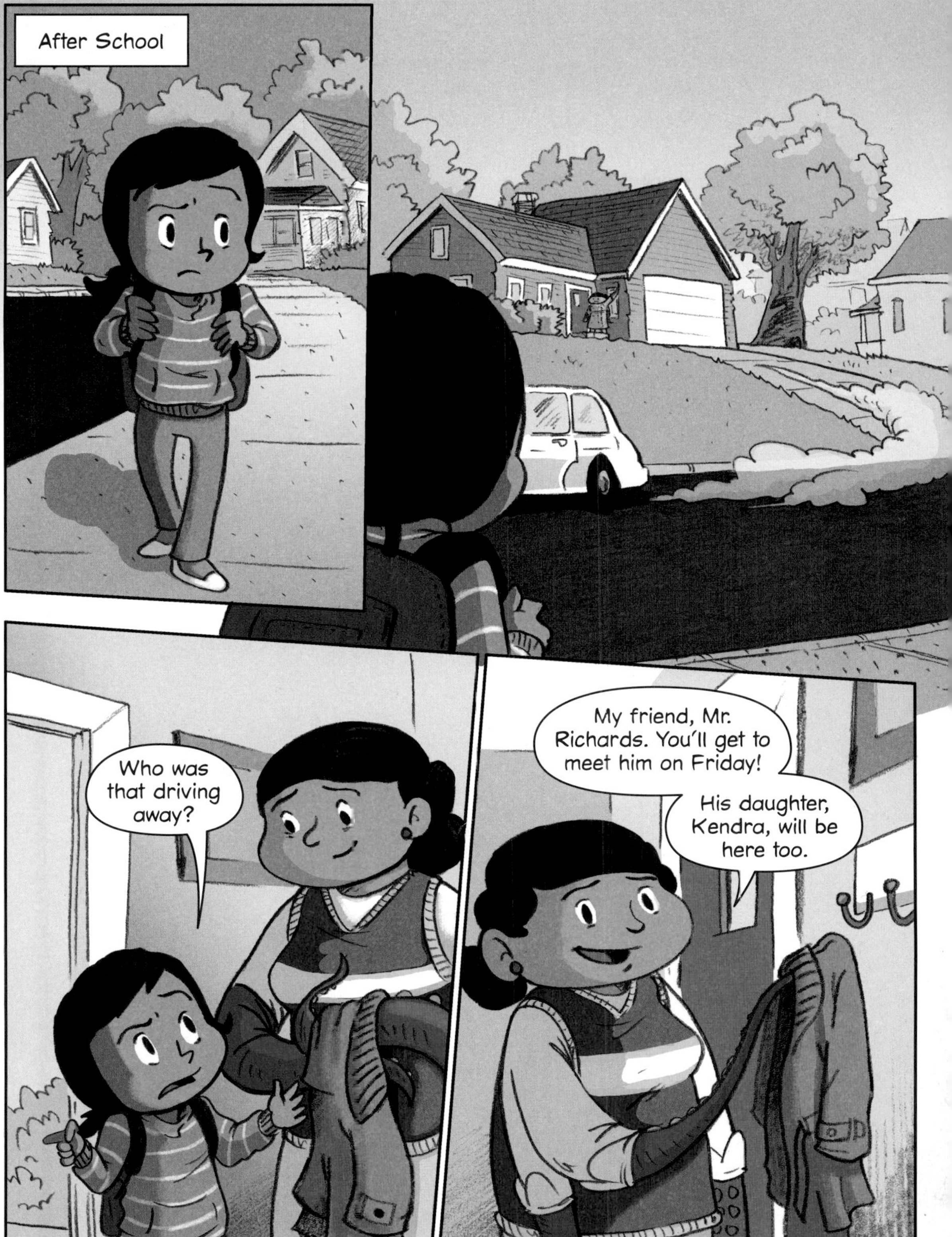
After School
Who was that driving away?
My friend, Mr. Richards. You'll get to meet him on Friday!
His daughter, Kendra, will be here too.

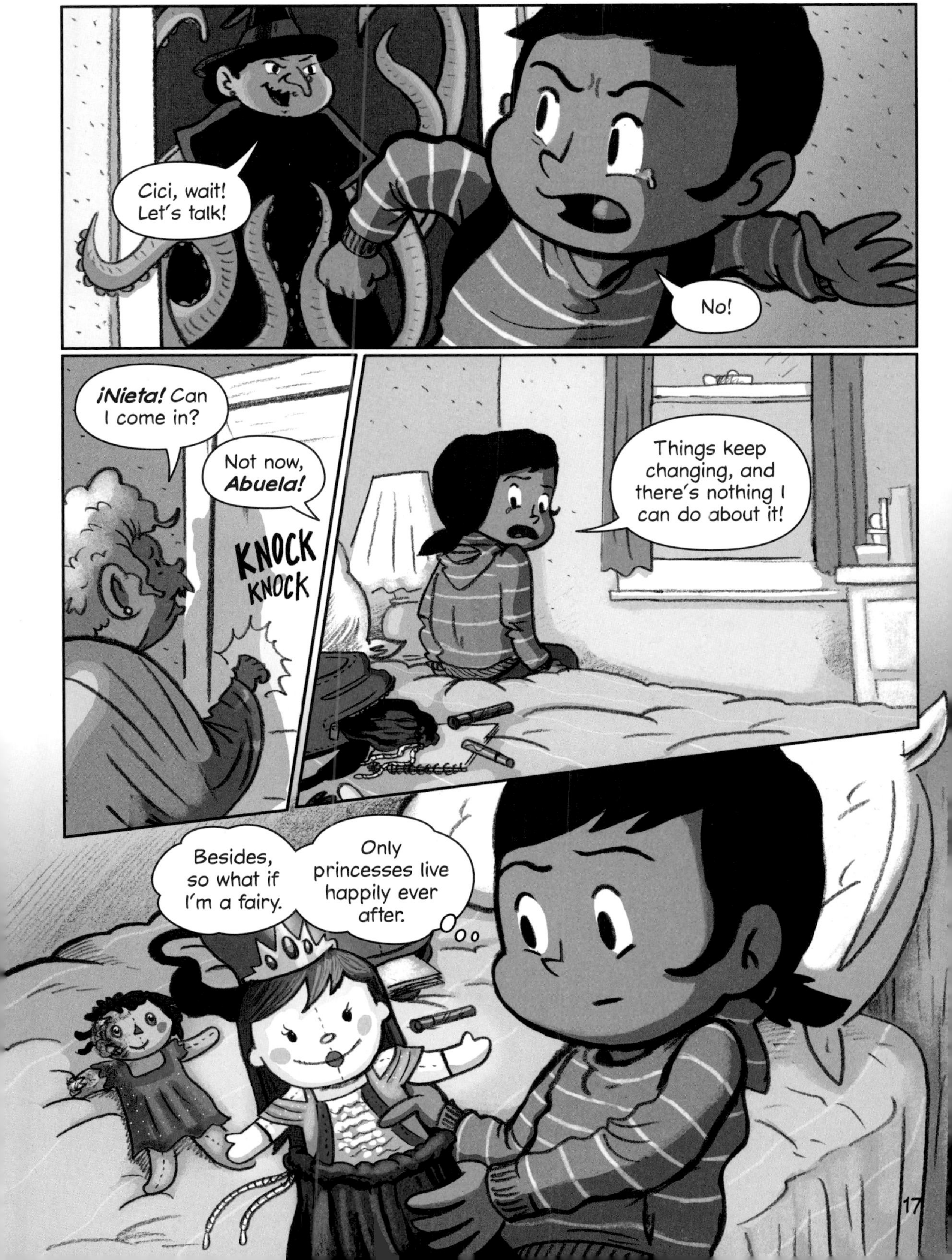

Cici, wait! Let's talk!
No!
¡Nieta! Can I come in?
Not now, Abuela!
KNOCK KNOCK
Things keep changing, and there's nothing I can do about it!
Besides, so what if I'm a fairy.
Only princesses live happily ever after.

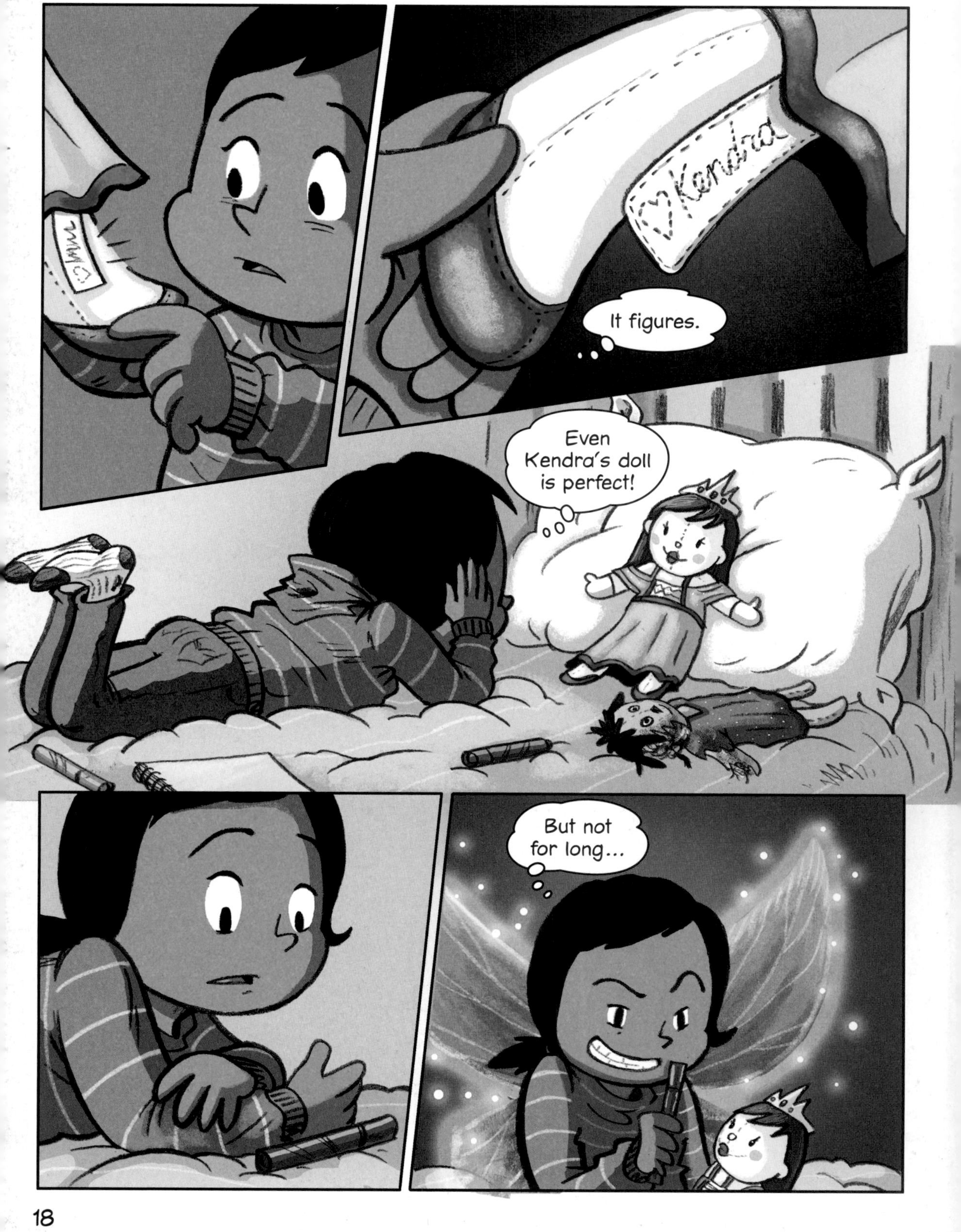
Kendra
It figures.
Even Kendra's doll is perfect!
But not for long...

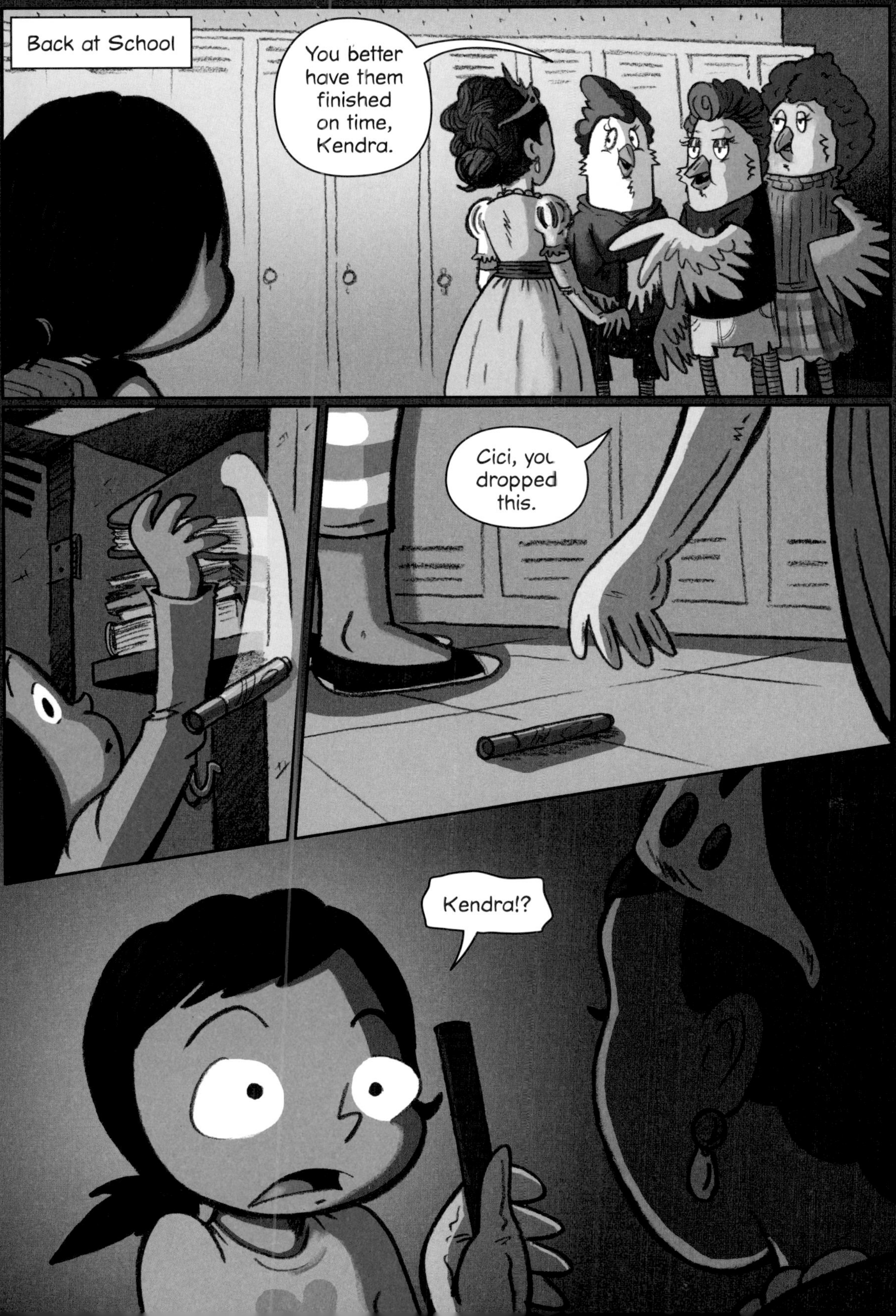
Back at School
You better have them finished on time, Kendra.
Cici, you dropped this.
Kendra!?

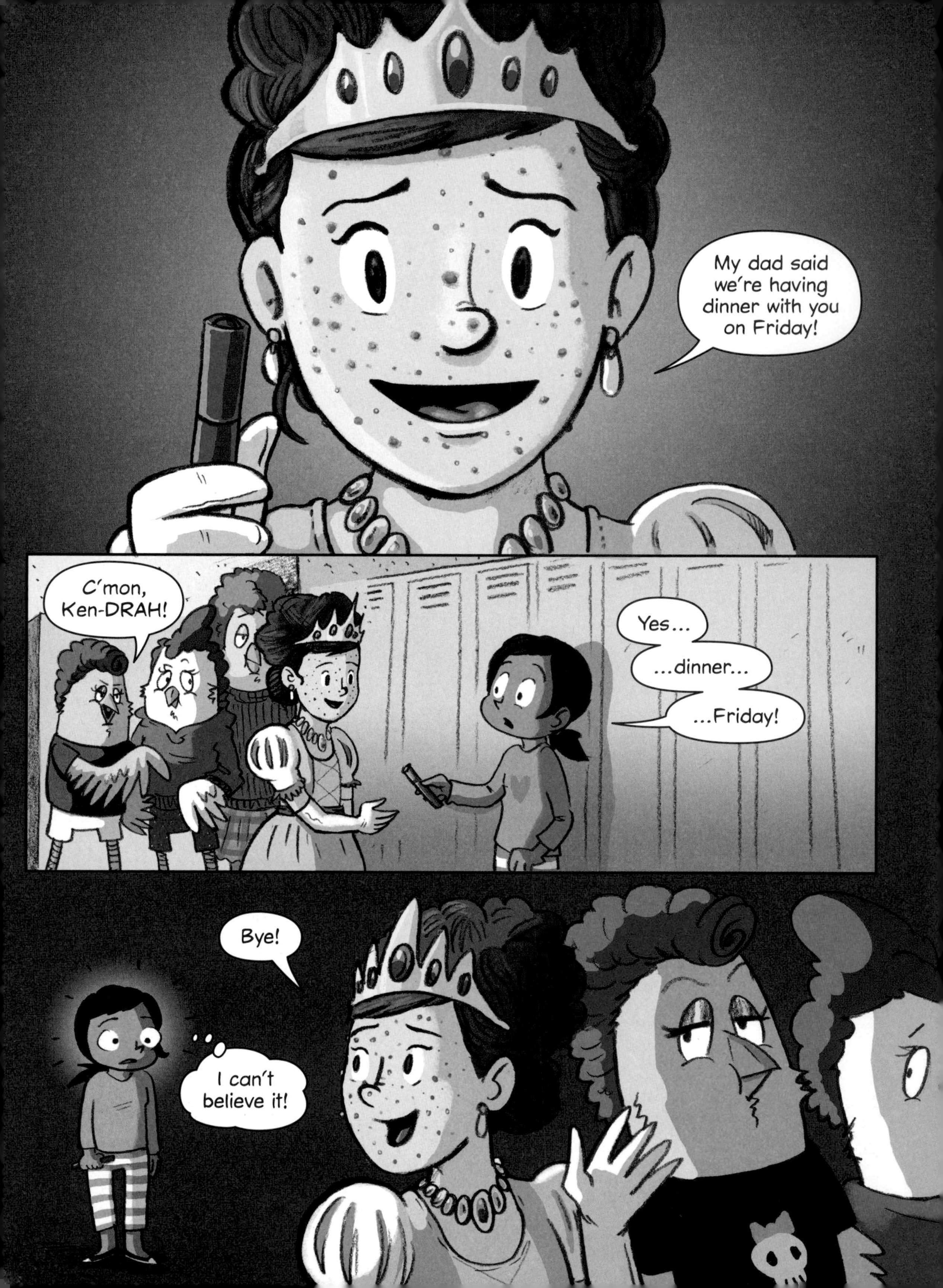
My dad said we're having dinner with you on Friday!
C'mon, Ken-DRAH!
Yes...
...dinner...
...Friday!
Bye!
I can't believe it!

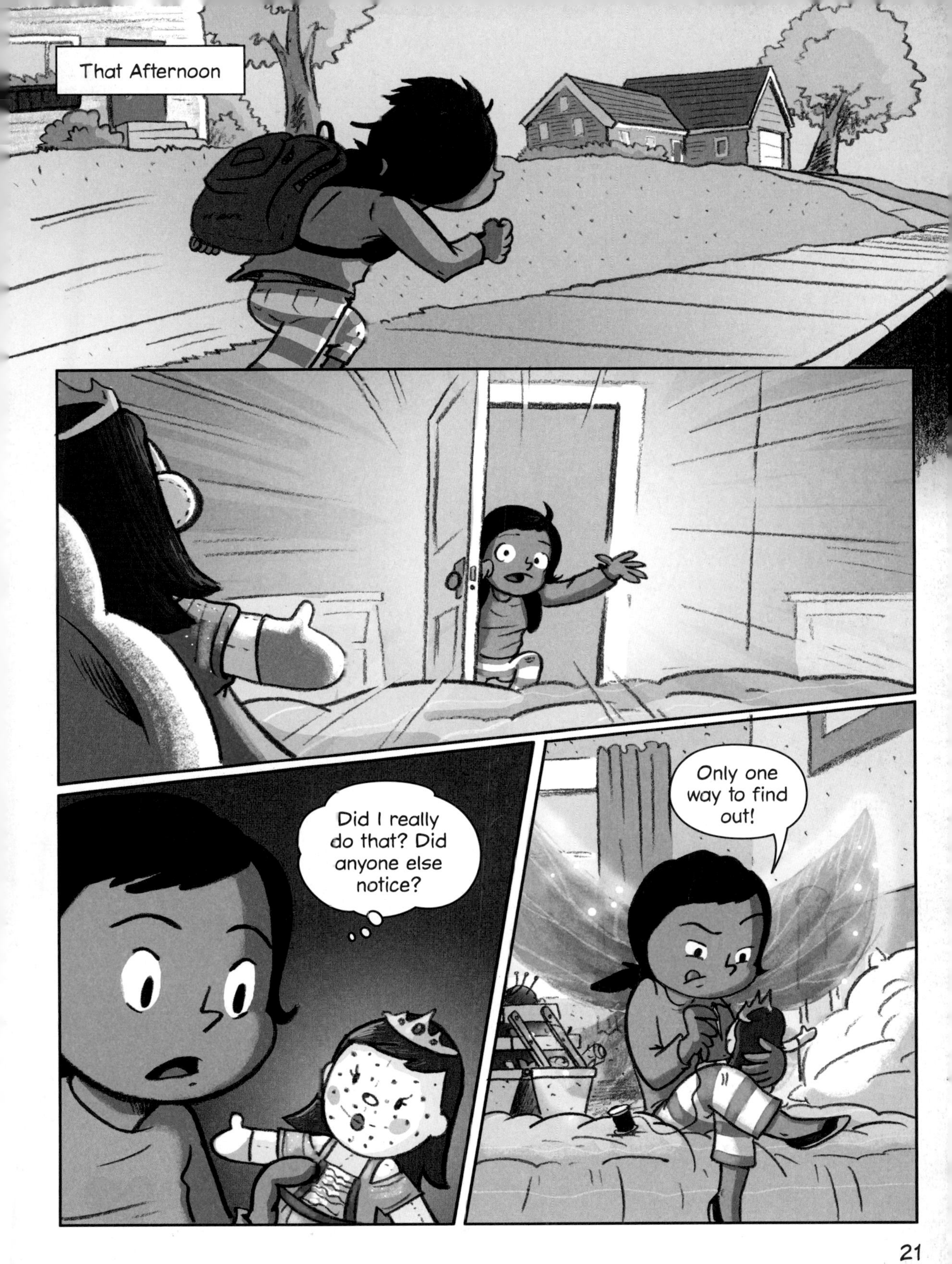
That Afternoon
Did I really do that? Did anyone else notice?
Only one way to find out!

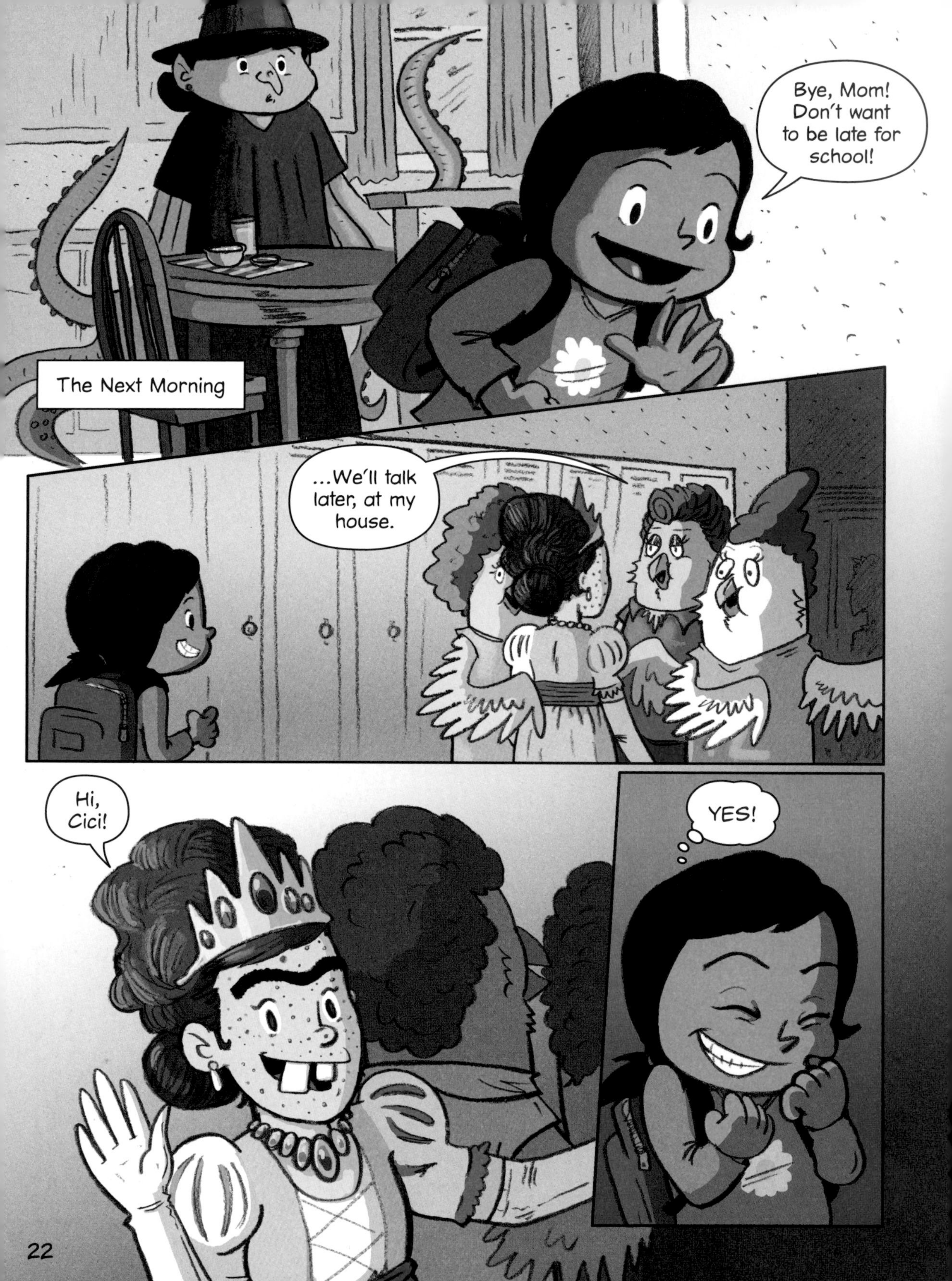
The Next Morning
Bye, Mom! Don't want to be late for school!
...We'll talk later, at my house.
Hi, Cici!
YES!

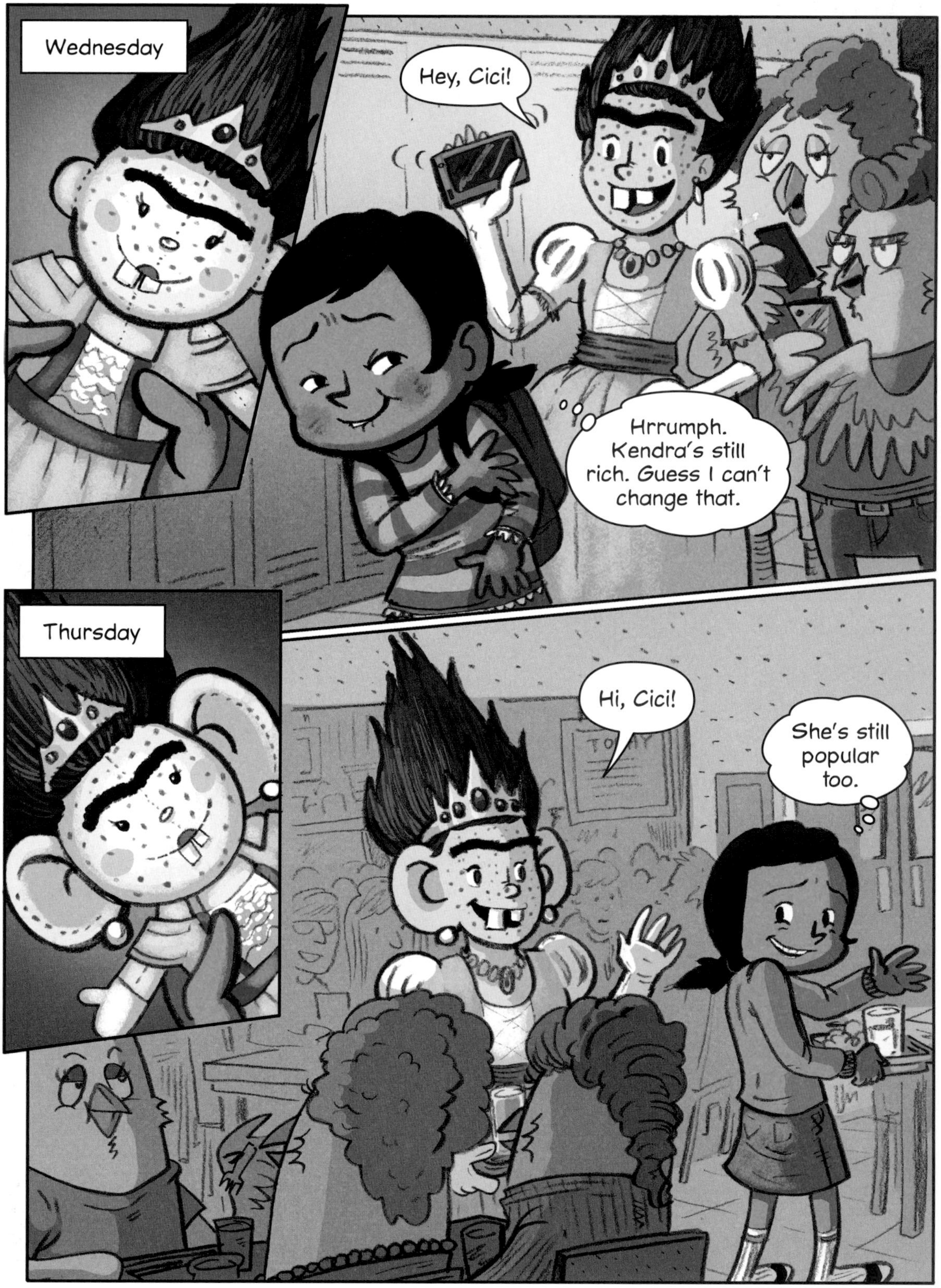
Wednesday
Hey, Cici!
Hrrumph. Kendra's still rich. Guess I can't change that.
Thursday
Hi, Cici!
She's still popular too.

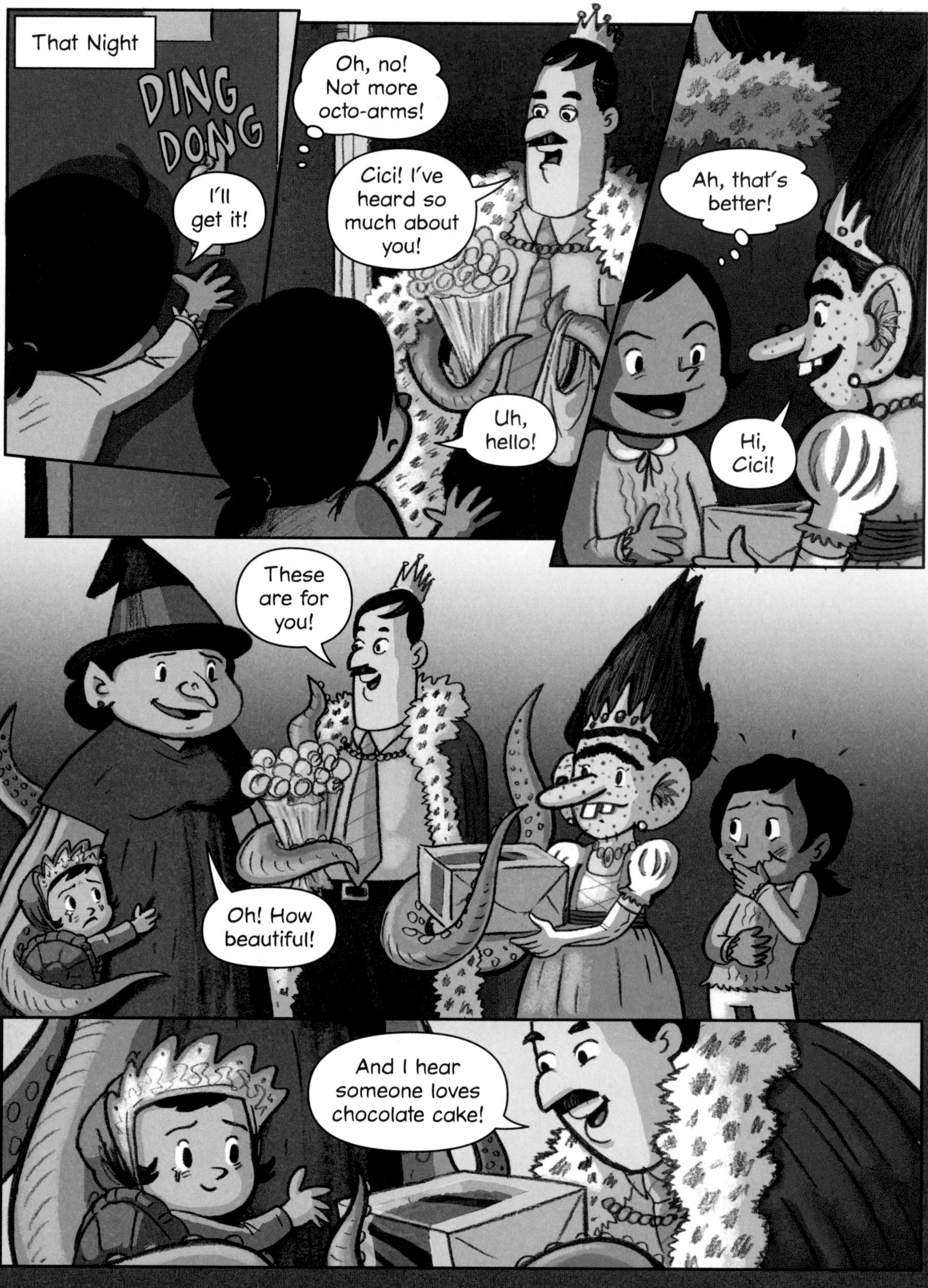

That Night
DING DONG
I'll get it!
Oh, no! Not more octo-arms!
Cici! I've heard so much about you!
Uh, hello!
Ah, that's better!
Hi, Cici!
These are for you!
Oh! How beautiful!
And I hear someone loves chocolate cake!

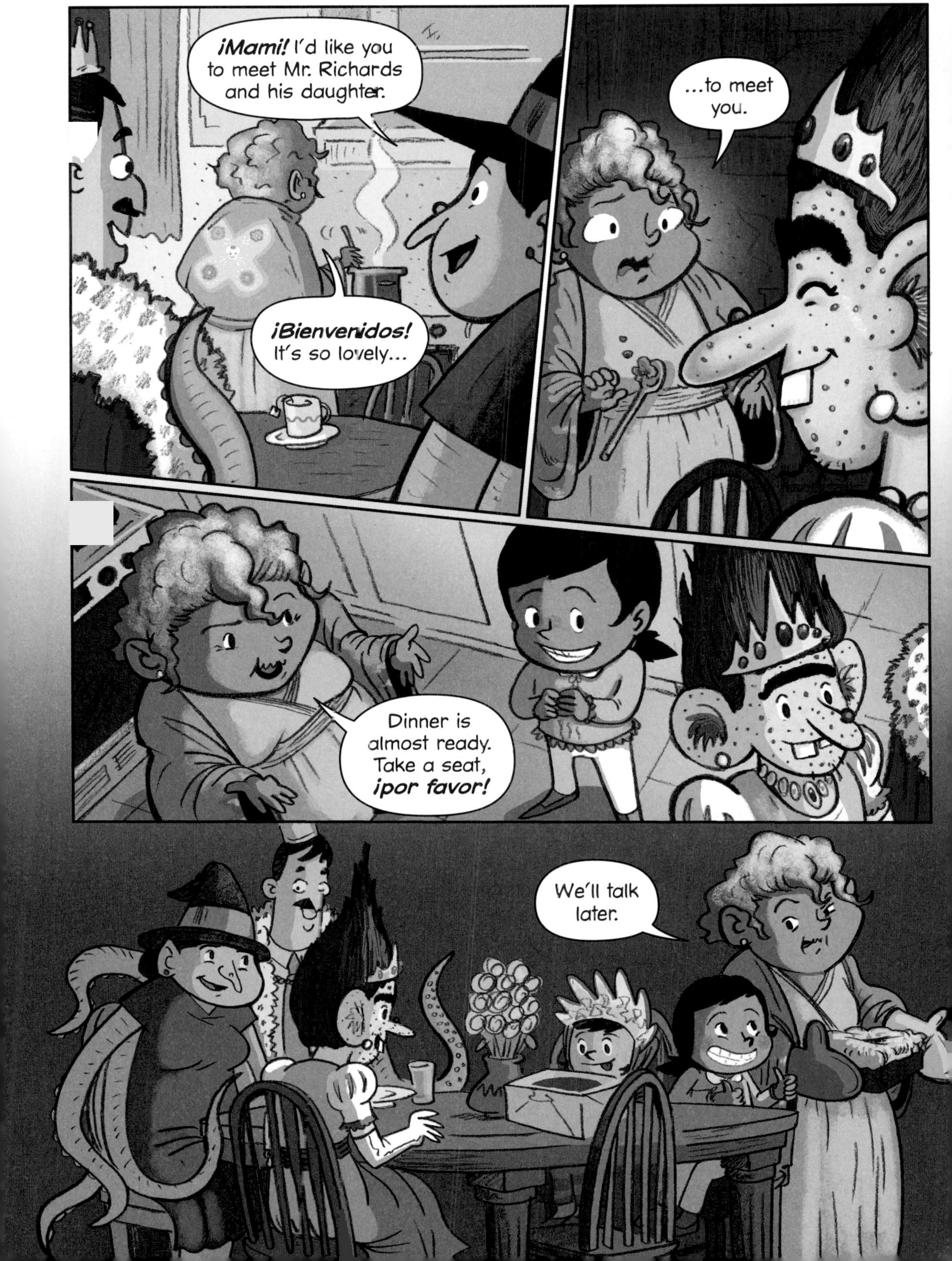
¡Mami! I'd like you to meet Mr. Richards and his daughter.
¡Bienvenidos! It's so lovely...
...to meet you.
Dinner is almost ready. Take a seat, ¡por favor!
We'll talk later.

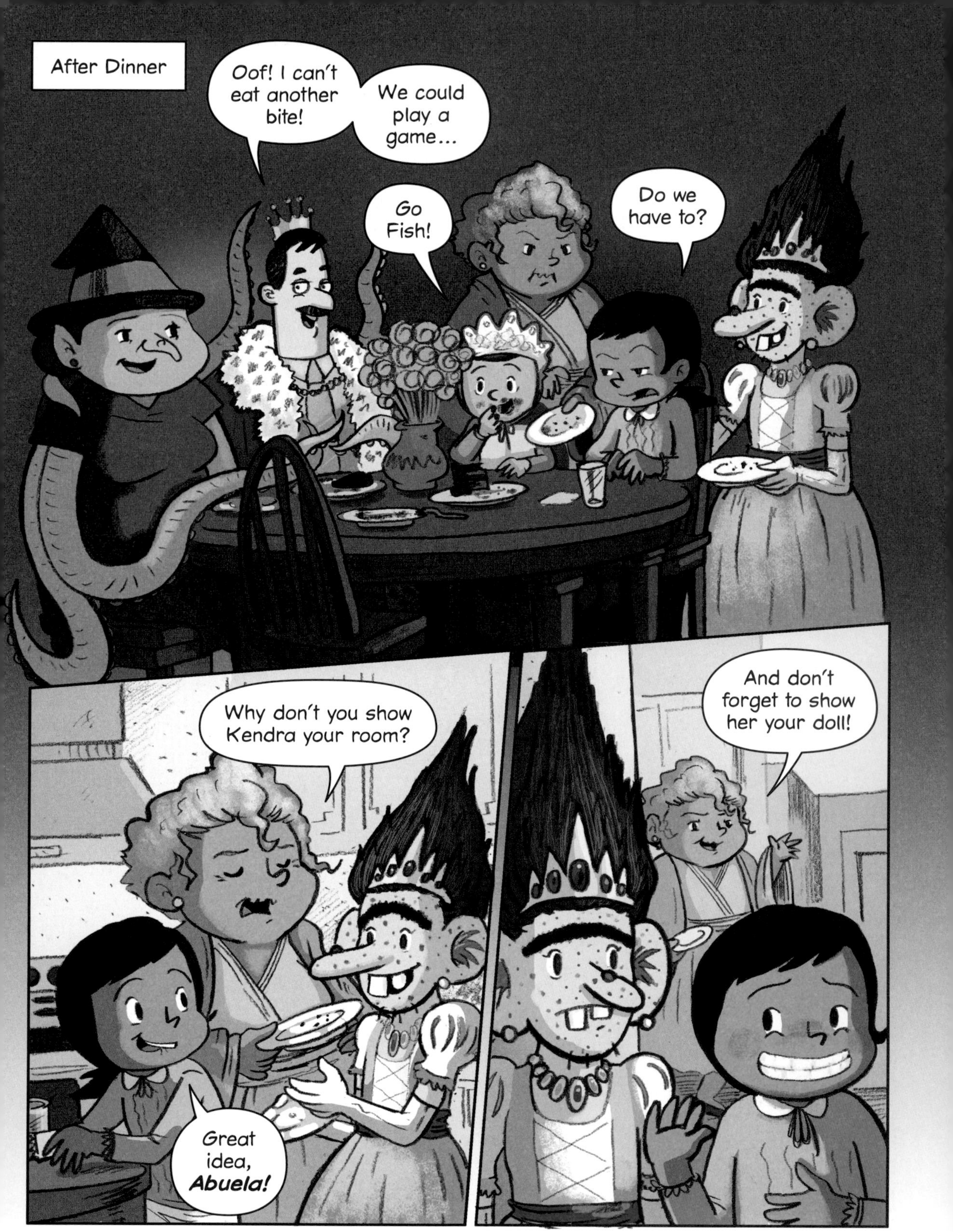
After Dinner
Oof! I can't eat another bite!
We could play a game...
Go Fish!
Do we have to?
Why don't you show Kendra your room?
Great idea, ***Abuela!***
And don't forget to show her your doll!

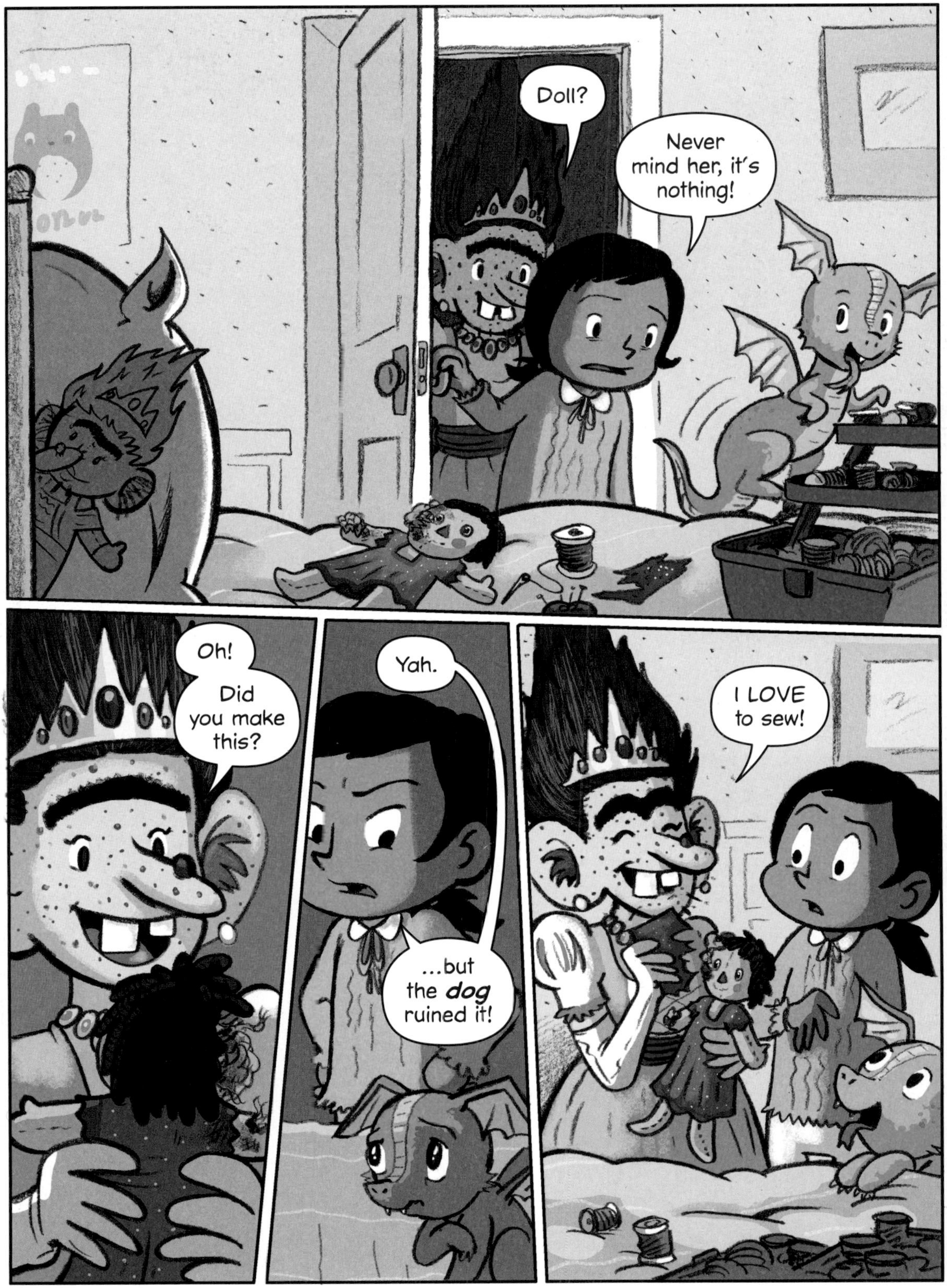
Doll?
Never mind her, it's nothing!
Oh!
Did you make this?
Yah.
...but the *dog* ruined it!
I LOVE to sew!

31

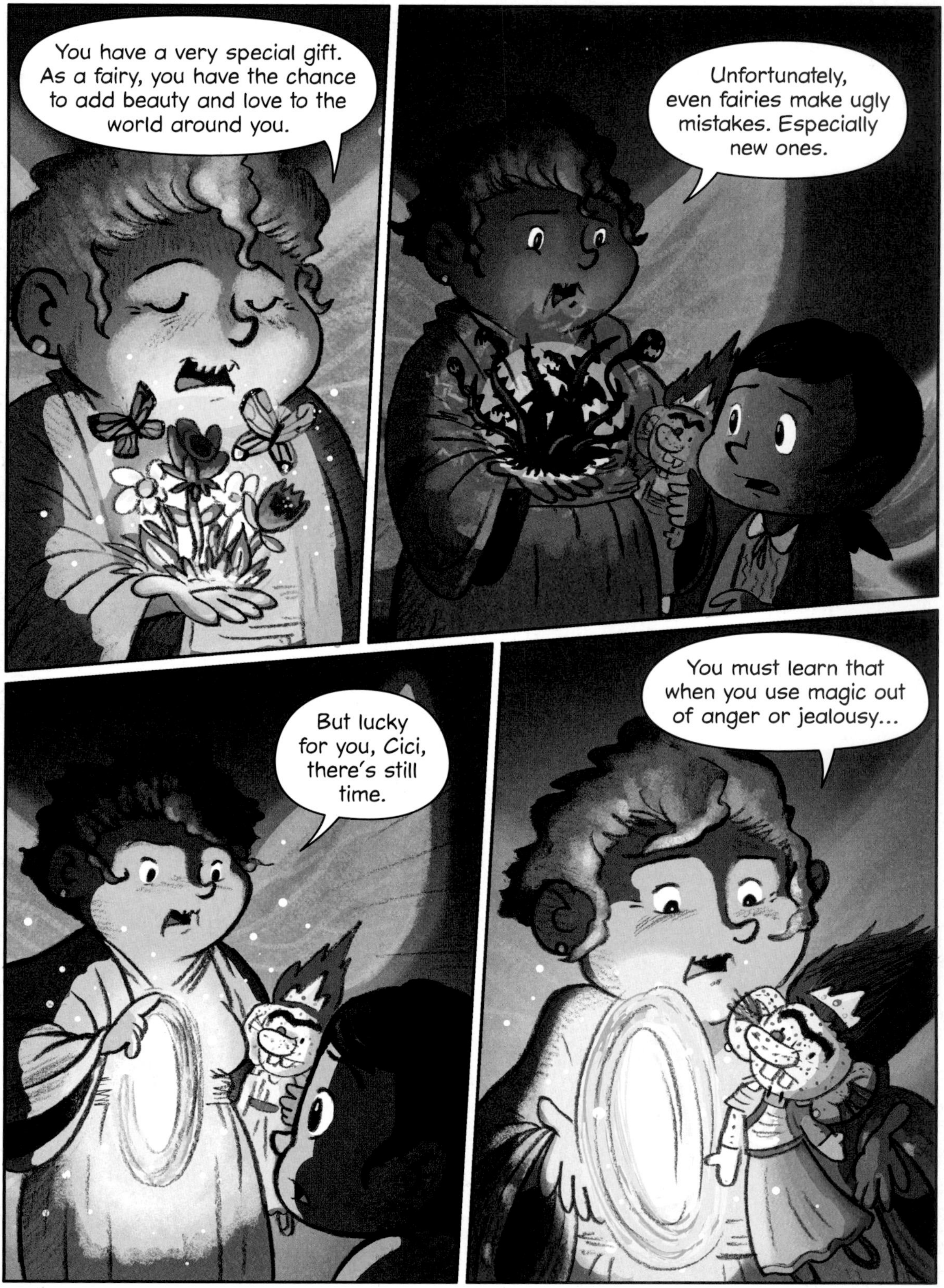
You have a very special gift. As a fairy, you have the chance to add beauty and love to the world around you.
Unfortunately, even fairies make ugly mistakes. Especially new ones.
But lucky for you, Cici, there's still time.
You must learn that when you use magic out of anger or jealousy...

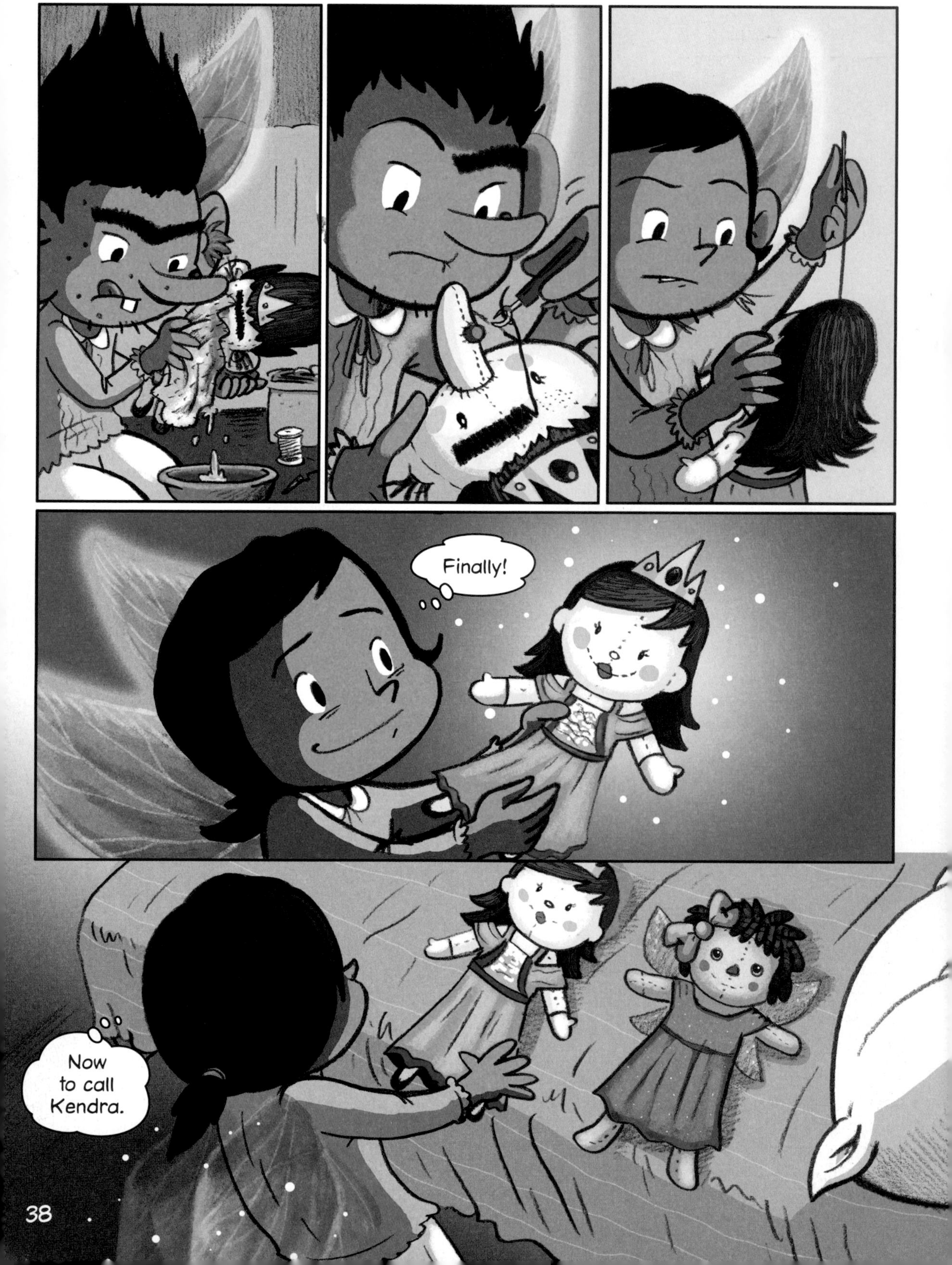
Finally!
Now to call Kendra.

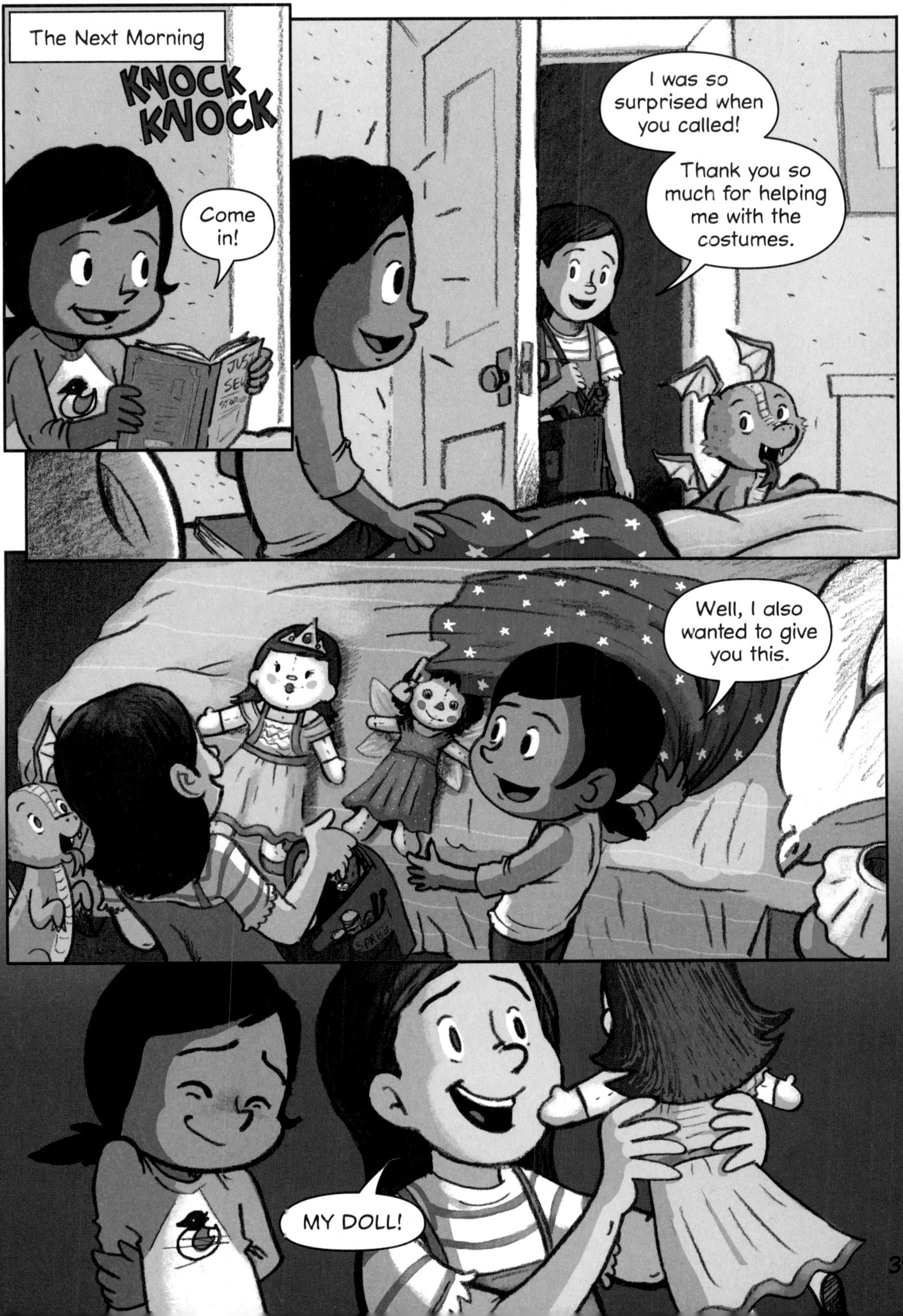

The Next Morning
KNOCK KNOCK
Come in!
I was so surprised when you called!
Thank you so much for helping me with the costumes.
Well, I also wanted to give you this.
MY DOLL!

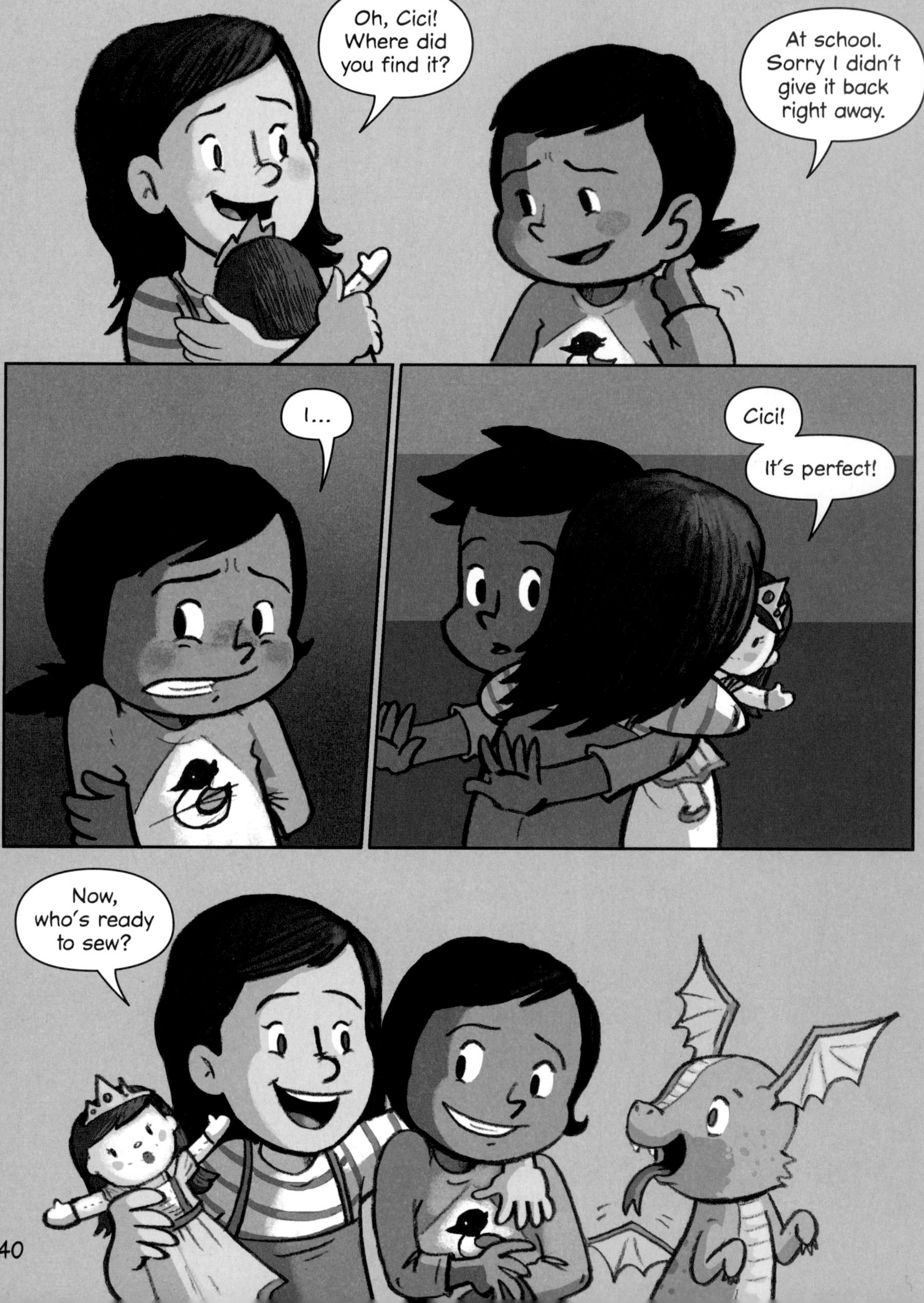
Oh, Cici! Where did you find it?
At school. Sorry I didn't give it back right away.
I...
Cici!
It's perfect!
Now, who's ready to sew?

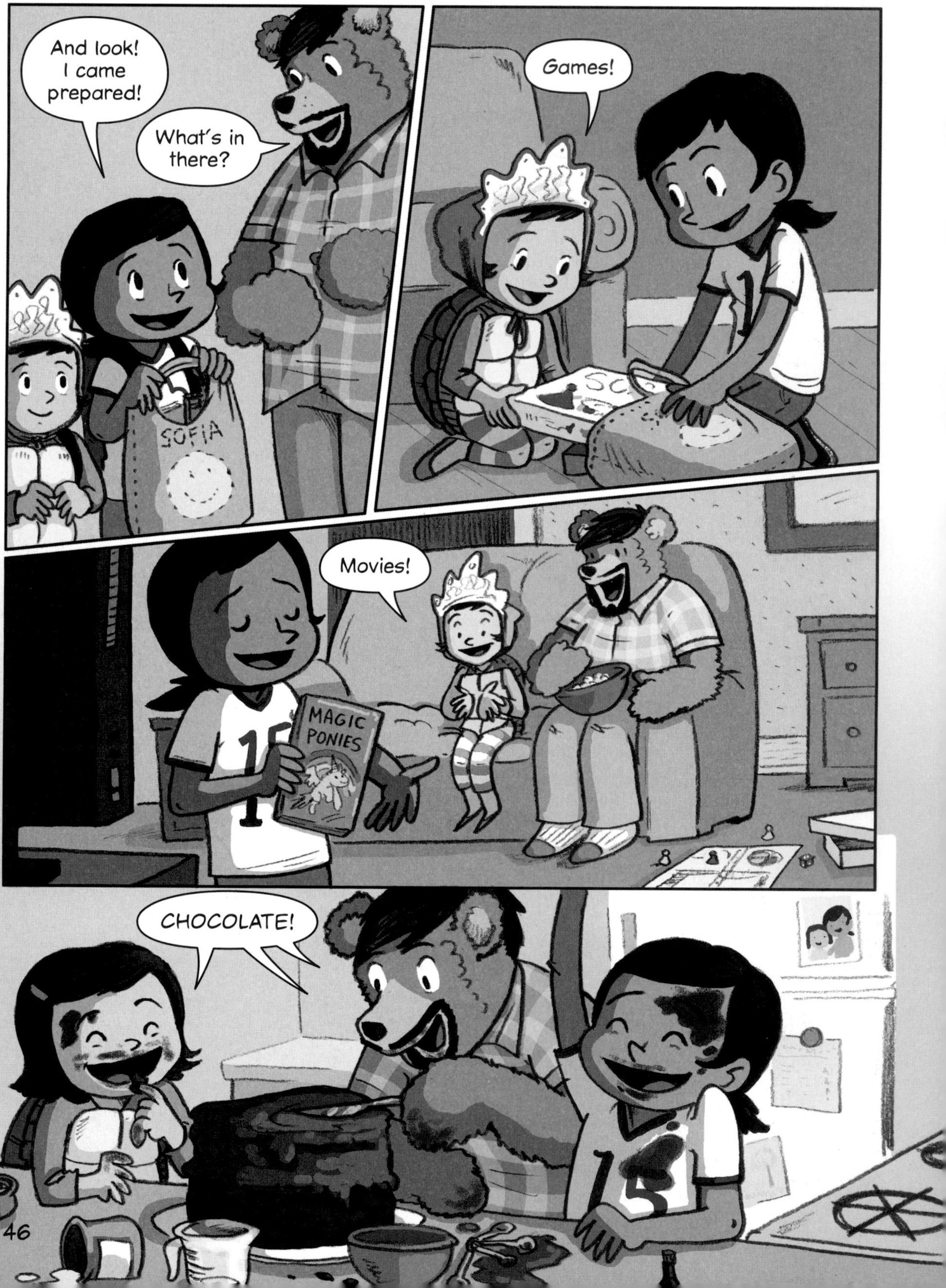
And look! I came prepared!
What's in there?
SOFIA
Games!
Movies!
MAGIC PONIES
CHOCOLATE!

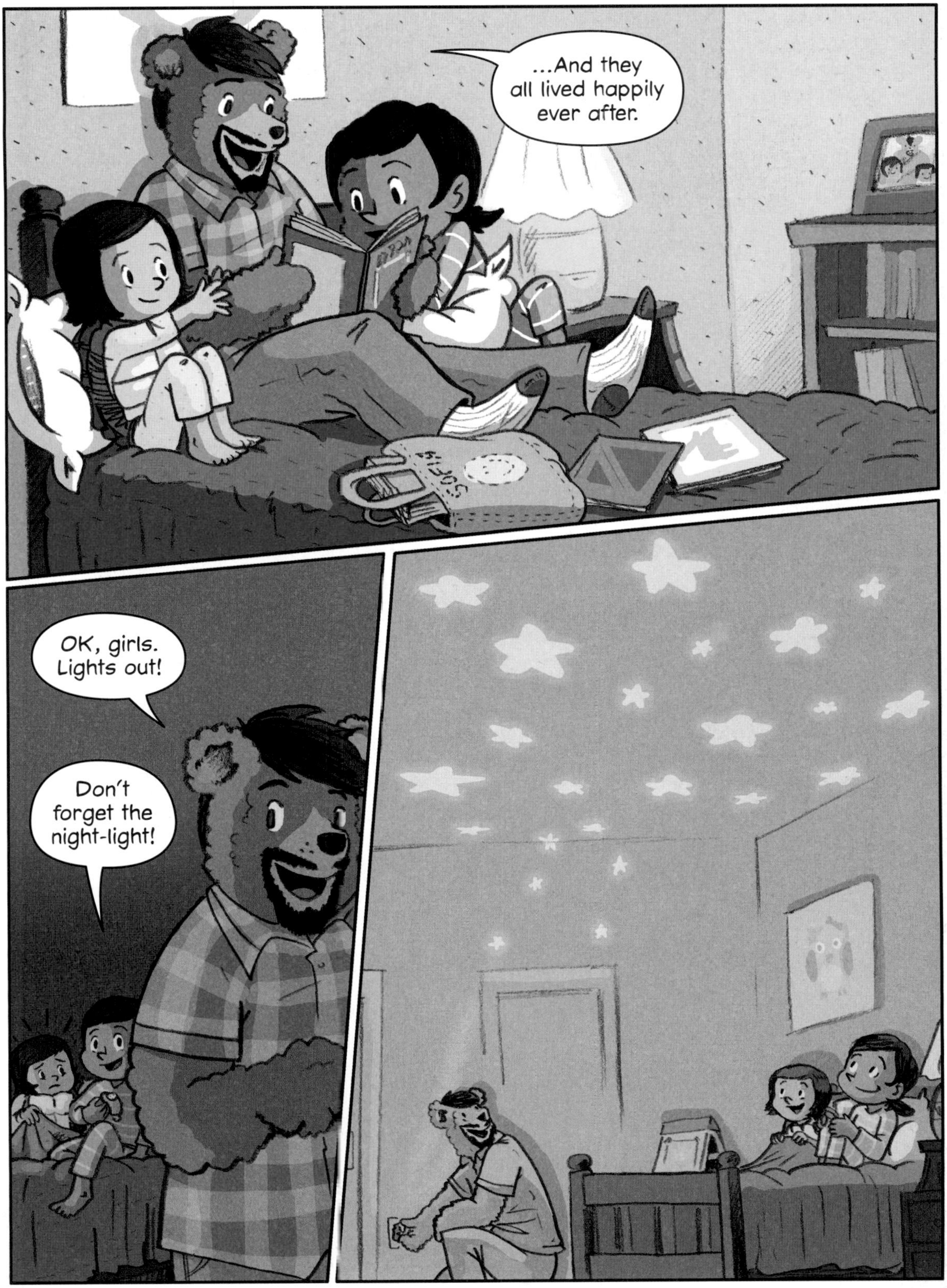
...And they all lived happily ever after.
SOFIA'S
OK, girls. Lights out!
Don't forget the night-light!